CITY OF KAUS

REVENGE

BOOK 1

FoxTales Press

DANI HOOTS

Revenge
City of Kaus, #1
First Edition © 2021 FoxTales Press
Edits by Victory Editing
Cover Art Copyright © 2021 Mona Finden
Cover Format Copyright © 2021 by Biserka
Designs

All rights reserved.

ISBN for Paperback: 978-1-956495-02-7
ISBN for Hardcover: 978-1-956495-01-0

"You must never give into despair. Allow yourself to slip down that road and you surrender to your lowest instincts."

—Uncle Iroh

CHAPTER I

<u>Ellie</u>

It didn't used to be this way.

I tapped my smoke on the ashtray, exhaling the herb-filled vapor. It was a delightful blend of local plants and made to order at the bar. This establishment seemed to have it all—smokes; drinks, both alcoholic and not; games; food; gambling. It was all here, meaning everyone in town occupied the small establishment at all hours of the day.

Thank goodness all I could smell was my herbal

what my kind appeared like as well, at least for the most part. I glanced around and found quite a few as humans liked to travel and settle among the different zones and then create half species, or half humans. Typical humans.

I sighed as I glanced around some more, seeing if I could spot my own race.

As if that were going to happen.

This was the new norm, I supposed. There weren't many of us Kausians left—shape-shifters who almost all had been destroyed in the attack three years ago. The other races didn't like us as we could turn into any creature or race we wanted. The only way to tell we were Kausians was with our shimmering gold eyes. Each zone used propaganda against our race, making it illegal for us to shift, and eventually we were attacked. The problem was, our zone was heavily armored and shielded. Someone had to have given them the codes and told them how to get in. I fiddled with the wooden ring that hung from my neck.

And that person was my ex, Cornelius Adams.

Zach brought me back to the present. "Not too many humans in these parts though, so he might know something. Surprised he didn't want to meet in the

Quarter."

That was fair. Humans typically stayed in the Quarter, which was across town. It was where all the humans usually stayed. Then the beach was just on the other side of the city and was full of shelters for the Sirians to live in. It had been so long since I'd gone out in the water for a swim.

Taking a deep breath, I reminded myself what happened the last time I jumped in water and how the Sirians tried to kill me for entering their area. They also didn't appreciate the fact I could turn into one of them. Live and learn, I supposed. At the time, I was only thirteen, so one would think they would be a little less aggressive about it.

I thumbed my 5Z742 revolver, which was named "Crazy Jack". It made me feel a bit safer when around all these distinct races.

"Well, well, what do we have here?" I heard a crackly voice to my right say.

I turned to find three Silurian men. They wore dark, scaly leather made of the large lizard creatures called Dracons they either used for meat, clothing, or rode instead of horses since horses couldn't hold up their weight. Only the Silurians could tame them, which I had a feeling had to do with the fact they appeared similar.

The larger of the three Silurians was the one to talk. He was more than likely their leader since they always went by who was largest. His eyes were almost at the side of his head, like a snake I wanted to shoot before it bit me. But in this crowd, I couldn't do that.

I gripped my gun, but kept it in my holster. "We aren't doing anything wrong, just enjoying some drinks. Go make trouble elsewhere." I turned and tried to ignore them.

One Silurian grabbed my shoulder and turned me back around. I wondered if there would be a day where I could go to a bar without getting harassed. That prospect was looking bleak.

"Don't you dare ignore me, you Kausian scum." His tongue slithered in his mouth, leaving me disgusted. There was nothing pretty about Silurians. Why couldn't I ever get yelled at by something handsome?

Zach stood up. "Hey, leave her alone."

"Oh, don't worry. I wasn't going to forget about you." The Silurian nodded for the other two to stand near Zach.

Glancing around, I noticed that most eyes were on us

now, and it didn't look like anyone was going to help. Typical. No one wanted to get involved if there were Silurians.

"We have a client we are waiting for, so unless you have business with us, meaning you will pay for our bounty-hunting services..." I flashed my gun at the Silurian. "... then it's best you leave us alone."

"Are you threatening me?"

"I'm only mirroring whatever your intent is, kind sir."

The Silurian hissed, glancing around me as if looking for some kind of weakness. If he ever ran into the few Kausians who were left, my gut told me they usually backed down or groveled at his feet by now. I, however, was not one to grovel.

I could see his long clawed hand reaching toward his leather belt, more than likely where he stored a weapon. Without a second thought, I pulled out my gun and shot him straight in the chest. I heard his two friends let out a screeching hiss. Pivoting, I shot the other two.

And then all hell broke loose.

For the record, I didn't use my actual bullets but some tranks. The lizards were only asleep—not dead. Bullets—as in real bullets that could kill—screamed out of there. We saved most of them by knocking them all out, but no one would see it that way.

I grabbed my smoke and left a few coins on the counter. I would not dine and dash.

"Uh, what happened here?" a voice said from the entrance.

Both Zach and I aimed our guns straight at the man.

He threw up his hands. "Whoa, whoa, whoa! I'm not going to shoot!"

We slowly lowered our weapons.

"Are you Elvira Ryder and Zachariah Richards?"

I gave him a once-over. He was human. Same in appearance as us Kausians except he didn't have glowing yellow eyes—that is, when we hadn't transformed. "Are you the informant?"

"Indeed I am. The name is Byron Hill." He glanced around. "Come with me. Let's go somewhere that's a bit more… lively."

"Most aren't dead, just stunned."

"Well, you will be dead if they wake and you're still here. I have a hideout in the Quarter. You won't be disturbed there." Mr. Blondie turned and led us out of the bar.

CHAPTER II

<u>Ellie</u>

Now that I wasn't afraid of being killed for the moment, I took another look at Byron. He was a lot more clean-cut than I imagined our informant to be and older, at least in his forties. He was a medium height, with blond hair and blue eyes. I wondered if he was a human or part of the Pleiadeans. Since he was in this establishment, I had a feeling he was one of the former. They also wore strange outfits, and he was wearing a typical suit—gray with some lavender accents.

I'd expected someone a little rougher around the edges, although looks could be deceiving. At first glance, I just looked like some older teen who likes leather boots, button-up shirts, and my hat, but really I was a bounty hunter—a successful one too. It was how I could pay for information on the whereabouts of Cornelius Adams—the man who destroyed everything we had ever had.

Zach, on the other hand, well, he was a superb shot; I'd give him that. But he appeared exactly how he acted. The two of us already stood out with our golden eyes, but he stood out even more with his ginger hair. Very few Kausians had that color hair, and those were ones who mingled with humans. Zach had told me he was half human when we were young, and I didn't really care. That never stopped other kids from picking on him, not to mention adults as well. I didn't understand how they could be mean to him as he was the biggest sweetheart I'd ever known.

"When we get to the Quarter, do you mind keeping your hats down a bit lower? I don't want to be seen with Kausians. You do understand, don't you?"

"We do," I answered as I pulled the brim of my hat down. I could still see the surrounding area and the few that were out as the two suns began to set. It was about fifty-fifty for whether Lyrans were more active in the night than during the day. It seemed that since many of the other zones interacted with them, they were no longer a nocturnal race. It was interesting how other cultures could change depending on their surroundings and relationships, but Kausians were never given that chance.

The Quarter was the name of any human district of the zones outside the Human Zone. Even Kaus had a Quarter in their city as humans were the only race that would interact with us. I always believed it was because we were most like them, minus the shape-shifting ability. I felt bad for the ones who'd lost their lives in the attack.

We came upon the Quarter, and different smokes and liquor fumes permeated the air, strong enough to cover up the smell of the ocean that filled the city. Men and women in ragged clothing sat on the corners, asking for money and performing tricks or playing some kind of instrument. That was one half of this area—the other half were rich men and women in fine suits and dresses who snubbed those who were either down on their luck or had been born into poverty. It was like this no matter which zone, but it seemed to me that it was only humans that had this big of a divide between the upper and lower class. Perhaps that was why humans always intermingled with other species—hoping for a better life.

It was never the case, however.

I watched as a man glanced around and pulled a wad of cash to hand to another gentleman. The man took it and guided the first man into the dark alleyway. Yes, this was definitely where the humans dwelled. Nothing legal ever happened behind those closed doors—or open doors, for that matter—and I felt a little safer since no security officer wanted to come to this area.

As we made our way through the Quarter, I noticed there were fewer people meandering on the street, and the buildings were a lot cleaner and well kept. Before long, we were coming across small mansions with front yards and gates.

This intel was going to cost us a pretty penny. I made sure Byron wasn't looking when I gave Zach a raise of an eyebrow. He gave me an equally perplexed eyebrow gesture. We didn't expect our information to come from someone as prestigious as this. It raised a few questions in my mind, but I decided not to ask them out loud.

We made it in front of one manor that had a large lawn of yarrow and statues of some humans—maybe his relatives or something. There were also a few fountains, which I found to be a waste of water, although I was from the desert and water scarcity wasn't as big an issue in the Lyran Zone. Summer flowers bloomed of every color one could think of and were cut and maintained very delicately.

We stepped inside, and it appeared exactly as I envisioned in my mind. Marble made up the flooring, and the walls were covered in a fancy red with wood that met it halfway up from the floor. Paintings that I imagined cost a fortune decorated the entry.

A human butler with dark hair and a tall stature came and helped us out of our coats and placed our hats on the coat hanger. I was capable of doing such things myself, but apparently Byron couldn't.

"Please take your seats in the lounge area. I'll be right with you." Byron went up the stairs.

I glanced over at Zach, who shrugged.

"I guess we should take a seat," Zach said as the butler gestured to the room. Once we were inside, the butler bowed and left our sight. Apparently, offering refreshments was only for those with stature. That didn't matter. I had enough to drink.

The room was a dark green, which contrasted the entry's red theme. There was a globe in the corner that marked the different zones on the continent that was Mu. Mu housed the five races and the rest of the world we were on, Maldek, which was mostly ocean or areas that weren't habitable. There was one fairly large island, but that was where the Pleiadeans lived, and they didn't like visitors, nor did they like leaving their home. They were similar to monks and wanted solitude, but at the same time, they would try to kill any who came close. It made no sense.

My eyes drifted some more, and I found used whiskey bottles, maps, and books littered the shelves along the walls. I tried to calculate how much they all would be together but lost count. Sitting on the green leather sofa, I took a deep breath. The air smelled of cigar smoke.

"I don't think we'll be able to afford his information, Ellie," Zach whispered. "And I don't think he'll give it to a charity case like us."

"I've been saving up for this day. Don't underestimate me."

"You've been holding out funds from me?"

I shrugged. "Here and there. Helps you stop buying such expensive drinks."

"But they are so good."

I rolled my eyes. But he had a point—the drinks he liked tasted like candy. I still preferred hard liquor, however, as for some reason it never left me with a hangover. It didn't make sense, but I decided not to look a gift horse in the mouth.

"Do you really think he has the information we need?" Zach asked as he leaned back and sighed. "I mean, after all this time? Did we finally find someone who has the answer to what we are searching for?"

"I think he does."

Zach glanced over at me from the corner of his eye. "And are you going to kill him when you find him?"

I clutched the ring that hung around my neck. That was the plan—I would take revenge on the man who betrayed me—who betrayed our kind. There was no repenting for what he'd done.

"I—"

"Sorry to keep you waiting." Byron came back into the room. Both Zach and I stood, but the man waved us to sit down. "You don't need to be so formal."

"Look," I began. "I don't care for small talk. What do

you know and how much?"

Byron grabbed a pipe and filled it with some ingredients and lit it. "It isn't a matter of money but more of what you will do for me."

I glanced over at Zach, and he nodded.

"Who do you want us to kill?"

CHAPTER III

<u>Zach</u>

Byron smiled and took a few puffs of his pipe after Ellie asked her question. I wasn't quite sure what to make of this guy. He seemed prim and proper, but we all knew that was a facade. The rich in the Human Zone were more corrupt than in any of the other zones— other than Silurians, of course, but that more had to do with them not caring about any race other than their own. This man before us probably had a lot of secrets— ones that not even Ellie nor I could dream of, and that sneak in, and kill. It was what we were good at, unfortunately. But I didn't want it to be our life, and neither did Ellie.

Laughter came from one alleyway we passed, and I quickly peered away as I did not want to see two people going at it. Sex wasn't something I felt comfortable around, whether it was other people discussing it or when it came to one's own needs. Ellie, I knew, lost her virginity to Cor when we were teens, and it made me realize I didn't have the desire, whether the other person be male or female. I felt there were more important things in this world, and I focused on those instead.

Like staying alive and not getting killed by bandits or law enforcers or both at the same time.

We arrived at our hotel and went next door to the horse stalls. My horse, Charlotte Hunkerbink III—Char for short, was a beautiful female Morgan horse with dark brown hair. She had been with me through thick and thin, and she meant the world to me. As I stepped up to her, she nuzzled me a bit.

"Who is a good girl, huh? Are they taking care of you here?"

"They better—we are paying a lot of money for them

to stay here," Ellie commented as she patted her horse, Kevin. Just Kevin. He was a speckled Marchador that had been with us as long as Char. He also helped us out of all the scraps we found ourselves in.

After giving them a good-night kiss, we made sure they had plenty of water and grass to munch on. Satisfied they were fine, we headed up the back stairs into our room.

Ellie was the first to collapse on the bed with a loud thump. Comfort came with money that neither of us had. We also never had enough cash for more than one bed, so we would cozy up. We had been friends since we were born and had plenty of sleepovers growing up. The past three years had simply been one sleepover after another.

"Ugh, move over. I want some bruises to wake up with too," I said as I set down the bullets and acted like I would collapse on her.

She laughed and moved over quickly. "Stop it! Don't lie on me."

I fell on the mattress next to her, but purposefully draped my arm and leg over her. She giggled some more and pushed me off. I rolled over and stared up at the ceiling that was stained with water spots and gods knew what else. I tried not to gag thinking about it.

"I should probably check to make sure there's no one hiding in the shower. Again." She sighed as she got up.

"Make sure to kill them promptly this time," I called after her. "We don't want a repeat of last week."

"Yeah, yeah." She stuck her head into the bathroom. "All clear. We are good to go."

"Or at least as good as it can be."

"You got that right." She jumped on the bed again.

"Hey, aren't you going to change?" I asked as she pulled back the blanket.

"Ugh, do I have to?"

"I don't want to sleep next to someone covered in filth."

She rolled back up. "Fine, but you need to change too."

I chuckled. "What are you talking about? I'm clean as a whistle."

"Yeah, right. Get your dirty ass off the bed." She grabbed my arm and pulled me up. I moaned as I stumbled over to my bag and pulled out my shirt and shorts I normally slept in.

"Next stop, I think we will have to do a laundry day. All my clothes are either caked in sweat, dirt, blood, or all the above."

Ellie slipped on a tank and her loose shorts. "Yeah, after we get the mark, we can go find a place to wash our clothes."

"Good." I put my own night clothes on and tucked my dirty clothes away. "I'm pretty sure you have worn that shirt five times."

"Like you are any better." She collapsed back on the bed and slipped under the blanket.

I turned off the light and hit my knee straight into the wooden table they'd placed in the middle of the room.

"Son of a bitch," I said as I stumbled into the bed. "Why do they always put the furniture where I will run into it?"

"Because they want to hear you cuss."

"Apparently," I whimpered.

She slapped her hand on my injury. "There, there, you're fine."

We lay there, silent. The sounds of either mice or the ghosts of all the people murdered in this hotel, or both, scratching at the wall made me wish we had a little more money to spend on lodging. I could hear Ellie's breath slow down as she was drifting into sleep. I turned to her, watching her mouth twitch in the city

three of a kind, which was he was betting I had.

Except I didn't—I had a four of a kind.

He added two black chips on the pile and looked over at me.

"Well then, lad, what says you?"

I ran my hand through my short, white hair. "You were talking such a game earlier. I can't let that all go to waste, now can I? I will call and raise you another black chip."

The old man stopped his winning quirk and glanced back down at the cards. I took a puff of my herbal joint as I watched him. It was obvious what he had, so for me to raise the stakes either meant I had the same thing as he, or I possibly had something higher. I could have been bluffing, of course, which I had done plenty of times this night. But he would have to bet his last remaining black chip to find out.

"I'll call." His voice broke a little, as he knew he was betting a lot on this game.

I shrugged as we both flipped over our cards. "Four of a kind. Sorry sir, today is not your lucky day."

The man stared at my cards. He couldn't believe it as he glanced at his hand, which was a jack and ten of clubs, and then over to my pair of fives. After a few moments, he started laughing.

"Well, I'll be. You are one heck of a player, young lad."

I didn't appreciate it when people called me a young lad—I was twenty-one now, and after the destruction of my kind, each day felt like a year.

The old man stood up. "Well, I am cleaned out. I bid you all a good night."

I nodded to him as he walked off and stacked my chips together.

Gabe shook his head. "I don't know how you do it. You're just full of luck, I swear."

"Maybe in cards, yes. Now, you came over here for a reason, right?" I glanced back at the dealer. "Can I get these chips converted please?"

She gave the equivalent in the least amount of chips so I could cash out.

"Thank you." I tipped her one of the smaller ships and then turned to the Sirian across from me and lowered my glasses a little to give her a wink. She didn't seem to care about my eye color as she blushed and licked her lips. Perhaps I was mistaken about her. I shifted to Gabe, who was just shaking his head.

"What?" I asked as we made our way toward the bar.

This wasn't my favorite parlor, although it was a nice one in the Human Zone. I just really hated all the blue. There was just so much of it—I could even make it out with my sunglasses on it was so vibrant. I noted that the bartender who stood behind the bar we were headed toward was wearing an all-blue suit too. I sighed and felt a little stupid, also wearing a blue button-up shirt, but at least I had dark brown pants.

"You get all the luck with money and women. It's not fair."

I laughed. "I guess you could say that." I wrapped my arm around his waist. "But it's thanks to you I get to be in this place anyway." I raised my free hand as if there was an invisible sign. "And next up, Zynon."

"I can't even imagine what kind of trouble you will cause up there this time. You know those big businessmen dislike it when they are beat at games and lose money. Go easy on them."

I sighed. "I'll try. It's not my fault I am lucky at gambling on top of my amazing skill. And what about you? They already hate that your trial period is almost up. Some of them aren't too keen on the fact you will be initiated in the coming weeks."

"Oh, I have a feeling a few of them will try to stop

me. That's why I'll have you head up there a few days before me and make sure no one is plotting to assassinate me."

We took a seat at the bar. At least the seats were comfy, even if they were an awesome aquamarine that clashed with the royal blue that covered most everything else.

"Barkeep, I will take a whiskey. Straight. Your second-best bottle please." I glanced to Gabe, who nodded. "Make that two."

The bartender—a human with blond slicked-back hair—nodded and grabbed a bottle from the top shelf. I noticed dirt under his fingernails. It was clear this wasn't his only job. It was sad how much of a divide there was from a commoner with a job or two, and the rich who I didn't quite understand where their money was coming from.

I turned to Gabe. "And what if they send someone while you wait here? What will you do then?"

He shrugged. "I think I can take them. I'm a lot more resourceful than you think."

"Mm-hmm."

"What's that supposed to mean? I've made it this far, haven't I?"

—Mother

I sighed as I crumbled the letter. She had found me. It was as if she couldn't take a hint. I was hiding from people and didn't need her giving away my location. Again.

It wasn't that I hated my mother—in fact, I loved her dearly. No, it was the fact that everyone at home loathed me and wished I was dead. I wasn't overreacting either as they frequently said it to my face. I left home a long time ago and never looked back, much to my mother's dismay.

I should call her, though, and get her off my back. Cor was busy, and he wouldn't know about it. He thought both my parents were out of the picture. I never said it myself, but he came to the conclusion himself and I didn't want to correct him. Grabbing my whiskey, I headed over to the public phones.

There were four phones, and luckily two of them were empty. One had a human fidgeting like crazy, begging the person on the other end to give him another couple of days. That didn't sound like it was going to end well. The other phone was occupied with a woman who was writing down some notes. I grabbed the phone on the end and put in a few coins since it would be long distance.

The phone rang three times before I heard my mother's voice. "Hello?"

"Hi, Mom." I let out a breath.

"Darling Riri, where have you been? I was worried sick!" Her melodious voice calmed my heart a little, even though I wished she hadn't found me this time— especially since that meant she might tell my father, who would in turn tell *him*. I also didn't like it when she called me Riri. No one but her called me that, and it was embarrassing.

"I'm fine. How did you find me?"

"Oh, you know how rumors travel. One of our dear friends saw you at that parlor you are staying at and told me."

I wasn't sure what dear friend that would have been, especially since all her friends hated me. She ignored that though and acted as if I were wanted with embracing arms.

"Well, here I am. Is there anything you needed?"

"I just wanted to know when you will be coming back to visit. I can get your favorite meals prepared and have a big ball welcoming you."

She just wanted to throw a party. I took a sip of my

whiskey. "I still have a lot to do. But don't stop from throwing a ball. Have at it."

"We are having one this weekend. Won't you come?"

"Sorry, I'm busy." Another sip.

"Well, next time then."

"Perhaps."

"…"

We really had nothing to talk about, which was one reason I rarely called her. "Look, mom, I've got to get going. It's late here."

"Oh? You have a partner, don't you? Cor, I believe his name was? When are you going to bring him home to meet the family?"

That was a good question—especially since he didn't know I had a family. "Later."

"Well, give me a heads-up. I want to make sure everything is ready for you."

"I will."

"Love you tons, Riri."

I took a chug of the whiskey this time. "Love you too, Mom."

I hung up and leaned my forehead against the wall. This wasn't good—this meant that people knew my whereabouts and would try to kill me. Then again, they always knew my whereabouts, so it really changed nothing. I guess Cor was right—I needed to learn to blend in more.

Standing straight up, I chugged the rest of the drink and took my empty glass back up to the bar. I needed another one of these or else I was going to suffer with some guilt I did not want to deal with.

Who was I kidding? No amount of drinking would make that go away.

But it sure numbed the pain a little. I took my seat again and waved to the bartender. Handing him the glass, I nodded to the bottle he had placed back on the top shelf.

"Can I get another?"

He took the glass as I melted back down on the table. I just wanted all this to be over. I smiled a little, realizing my mind just worked in circles. I couldn't stop the cycle now, could I? I needed to learn to be patient, but that was easier said than done.

I heard the bartender put the drink down beside me, and I slowly reached for it, the glass feeling cool against my fingers. I tapped my finger against it, listening to the click of my nail.

"You all right?"

Raising my head, I found a charming young woman standing next to me. She had long curly blond hair that was pinned up in back with a green hat that matched her dress. Black velvet was intricately sewn into the green, adding depth and design. If I had to guess, the dress cost more than the bartender got in tips over a month, if not five.

I smiled at her. "I'm fine. Just a lot on my mind."

"Mind if I sit?" she asked as she gestured to the chair.

I motioned her to go ahead. "This is a free place. Do as you will."

"Thank you." She sat down and took her dark gloves off. "I have seen you around here for a while, haven't I?"

She stared at me with her crystal-blue eyes. They reminded me of my father's.

"Yeah, I have been here for a week now."

"Not many stay in this place for that long a time. Do you have business in the zone?"

"Something like that."

"I like coming here every once in a while. Gambling is sort of a hobby of mine. I know most women don't care for it, but it is a lot of fun."

"I agree. Games are fun. I think more people should

enjoy them.''

She smiled a little as the bartender came over to get her order. She ordered a mimosa. Turning to me, she held out her hand. "I just realized I haven't formally introduced myself. My name is Elizabeth."

I shook her hand. "Gabriel."

The bartender set down her mimosa. She grabbed it and held it up. "Well, cheers, Gabriel. Here is to games and gambling."

I clinked my whiskey glass against her flute and watched as she took two big gulps of her drink. She licked her lips as she set her glass down.

"Speaking of games..." She placed her hand on my leg and moved it upward. "How about you and I go have a little game of our own? I will give you a discount."

I chuckled as I moved her hand away. "Sorry, you aren't my type."

She grabbed her mimosa and downed the rest. "Well, I will try my luck somewhere else."

"I'm sure you will find someone." I pointed to the other side of the parlor. "I think you will have the best luck over there. Trust me, that woman might be flirting with those men at the table, but she is more interested in someone of your caliber."

Elizabeth glanced back at me. "You know your stuff."

"I just tend to be quiet and notice things. But sometimes I am completely wrong."

"Well, I will try my chances. Have a good night."

"You as well."

I sipped my drink and motioned to the bartender. "Another please."

It was two hours before Cor came downstairs. He was smiling as he always does after he gets laid, or was he the one doing the laying? I started giggling at my joke as I downed another gulp of whiskey. I was funny.

Cor caught sight of me and made his way through the parlor. He saw the glasses in front of me and rubbed his forehead.

"Shit, Gabe…"

I swung around, my arms making the movement even larger, and smiled. "Cor! You're back!"

Cor glanced around to find others looking at us. "Not so loud. Come on, we need to get you in bed. But first…" He grabbed the drink I had in front of me and downed it. "One more for me."

"Hey! That was mine!"

He rolled his eyes. "No, you've had enough." Cor wrapped his arm around me and guided me toward the stairwell. "I don't want to deal with Hangover Gabe in the morning."

"You know as well as I, I don't get hungover." Even I could hear my words slurring. How much had I drank? Or was it drinken? Drunk? Why was that word so hard? "I drank a lot of water, so I should be fine.

"Whatever. Let's just get you to bed, all right?"

I smiled. "I could have gotten into someone else's bed I'll have you know?"

"Oh?" Cor didn't seem to be surprised. "And who was that?"

"Some girl named Elizabeth." I peered down the hallway to find a familiar green dress. I pointed. "Hey, that's her now!"

Elizabeth glanced over her shoulder, and I found she had been busy making out with the woman I had pointed out earlier. So I was right. I gave her a thumbs-up as Cor forced me farther up the stairs to the next floor.

"Well, I'm glad to see that worked out for her."

Cor shook his head. "Why can't Drunk Gabe be

quieter?"

"Because Drunk Gabe is happy!"

He laughed as he led me to our floor and toward our door. Most of the people who were going to hire prostitutes were already in their rooms, so there weren't many people around. Cor unlocked the door and half-heartedly threw me on the bed.

I frowned at him. "Hey, not so hard. I'm not like your clients."

"I barely threw you. Besides, a lot of my clients don't like the rough stuff unless they are delivering it to me."

I moved my head up to look up at him. "Speaking of which, how was tonight?"

Cor worked at his tie. "I'm not telling you. You get way too jealous when I give you details."

I pouted. "But I'm your handler."

He stepped on the bed, his knees on both sides of my waist. He bent down and kissed me. "And yet you get drunk after I go up and meet them."

I grasped Cor's collar and pulled him in closer. "But I know one thing for a fact."

He unclasped his belt. "And what's that?"

I pulled off his sunglasses. "I'm the only one who gets to have you in your true form."

Cor blushed, which surprised me. I had never asked him to change because I liked him for who he really was. He had suggested it, wondering what kind of human or humanoid I would be into, but I always just wanted him. Cor bent down and kissed me, the taste of whiskey still on both our mouths.

CHAPTER VI

<u>Ellie</u>

I was right. Zach was a lightweight and was completely hungover the next morning.

I woke up to find him sprawled across our small bed, his arms and legs draped over me. I blew his long red hair off my face as I tried to shove his body off me.

"Zach, wake up. We've got to head out," I shouted in his ear.

He moaned and held his hands to his ears, which left only his legs to move. "Why are you always so loud in the morning? My head is pounding."

I sighed. "Which is why I told you not to drink all those frilly drinks. You never listen."

"But they don't have that much alcohol in them." He rolled over, and I was free.

How many times had we been over this now? I had lost count. I got up and headed toward the shower before he had a chance to wake. Hopefully by the time I was out, he'd have come to his senses and started getting ready.

Because we were close to finding Cor.

Once we finished the missions, which should be easy enough, we would get the location of our friend, who not only stabbed us in the back but also brought down our entire species. It was because of him we had to endure life on the road, never settling and having to take bounty hunter jobs to survive. There weren't many Kausians alive—at least not that I could tell. It was rare to find any in the city as the locals made our life a living hell no matter what zone we were in. As for the rest of the wilderness, well, it wasn't easy to live where the bandits liked to attack.

I let out a deep breath as I turned on the shower. I waited for the brown ooze to become as clear and water-like as it would get and stepped inside. I could not wait until all this was over and Zach and I could find a tiny house in the middle of nowhere. Then the water wouldn't be contaminated by the city plumbing. Since we didn't have to pay for the info on Cor, that meant I had quite a bit saved up for it. Then we could plant a garden and live off the land.

Until some scoundrels came and messed it all up. Again.

But I was stronger now and better with a gun. We would simply keep a stockpile of bullets, and I doubt anyone would mess with us this time.

I quickly lathered myself with the soap that smelled of strong patchouli and washed off. The soap wasn't the best quality, which meant that I still felt slimy no matter how many times I rinsed.

Giving up, I turned the water off. Zach also needed to take a shower, and I had a feeling there wasn't too much warm water for each of these rooms. I could barely get it to a comfortable temperature as it was, and I doubted many people were already awake in this hotel. The first sun had just peeked itself up over the horizon, and during this season of the year, the second sun would come up in about two hours. I wanted to get as far as I could before the second one came up and made the day even hotter.

Stepping out of the shower, I found Zach cradling some water, staring at it with his golden eyes.

"Nice to see you're up," I said as I changed into some of the cleaner clothes I had.

He grimaced. "Not so loud."

"If you thought that was loud, you will have one hell of a time on a horse all day. Go take a quick shower, and we can get you a nice greasy breakfast."

He nodded and staggered to the bathroom. He did this every time we had a mission, I swore.

As Zach took a shower and got ready, I packed the rest of our things and left out his cleanest outfit. He was right last night; we needed to do laundry soon. After we assassinated the target, we would find somewhere that would let us wash our clothes. Since we were going to the Human Zone, it would be easier. A lot of places didn't serve our kind, or the other customers would try to ruin our clothes by throwing a red sock into our whites and so on. I had pink shirts for ages.

The last thing that was left to put on was my necklace.

It wasn't so much a necklace as it was a leather string

with a wooden ring attached. I took it from the nightstand and lifted it over my head so it could be tucked safely under my shirt. I peered down at it, running my thumb over the inscription in Kausian.

FOREVER

What a load of shit that was. I tucked it away and finished getting everything ready. We didn't have much in the way of stuff, but what we had was all our lives put together, and it fit in a couple of bags. Once Zach was done, we could grab some food and be on our way.

I sat on the bed, and it creaked as much as it had during the night. At least right now I wasn't trying to sleep. I tried to take some deep, therapeutic breaths as I waited for Zach. I tended to work myself up in the mornings, mainly when I put my ring away, so I was instructed to calm myself down. It wasn't my fault, it brought up painful memories, but it wasn't exactly like I could get rid of it—it pushed me forward to get revenge for our kind.

Another deep breath.

Zach came out of the bathroom and seemed better than earlier, but his eyes were still red and he had some dark circles. He changed slowly, as if each motion hurt him. I threw his bag at him, and he grimaced something fierce.

"Ready for some food?"

We found a diner close to the hotel, which was perfect since then we wouldn't have to travel far back to retrieve our horses. The two of us split an enormous breakfast platter of eggs, ham, sausages, bacon, hash browns, beans, tomatoes, mushrooms, and blood sausage. Then, of course, we both had some tea and toast to go with it.

The meal was oily, full of protein and fat, and perfect for helping Zach get over his hangover. After a few bites, he was acting like his old annoying self.

"The humans always make the best food, I swear!" He patted his belly after he finished his last bite.

"Yeah, well, because they are the most like us in regard to natural body type, even if we can change forms. Although I have to admit their food is a little too sweet and meaty for my taste. Every once in a while is fine, but I think I'm good on meat for a while."

"It's better than those protein bars we are always eating."

I shrugged. "They have all the nutrients we need to

survive, and they are filling."

"But they don't satisfy like this does."

He had a point, but we couldn't afford to eat out all the time. I only chose to eat here since we didn't have to pay for the information we saved up for and because I didn't want to deal with Hungover Zach all day. "Whatever. We better head out before the second sun is up. And before those fellows from yesterday find us."

Zach nodded. "Right. I forgot about them. I'm just so used to always having to leave town because you get into a fight."

I gave him a look. "Yeah, right. You were there too. It wasn't my fault people keep coming up to me and wanting to pick a fight. It just happens."

"You have an aura, Ellie, one that says 'come and fight me, bitch.'"

He had a point. "Fair. But we still better hurry. We will be pushing it to try to get there in a week's time. Lucky for us we don't have to take the train."

"Is it really that much of a problem taking the train, Ellie? We don't get saddle sore. We can just chill."

"Chill? We never get to chill on the train, Zach. There's too many people who always notice us and start picking a fight. Then we get thrown off and have to walk all the way to the nearest town and hope to the gods they don't have wanted signs of us."

He shrugged. "Fair. I guess riding our horses across the land will be safer. You know, with all those bandits and whatnot."

Zach had a point there. "Let's just take the horses. It will be easier. I don't want to deal with any more people."

"Fine, fine. But next time, we are taking the train."

"Deal."

We finished eating and went shopping for supplies for the next week. Mostly we needed food and water, although we knew which streams were safe to drink from as this wasn't the first time we had ridden from the Lyran Zone to the Human Zone. After we were done, we headed toward the stables to retrieve our horses.

Most people were already out and about, getting supplies, food, or heading to work. I watched as a mixture of species went about their day, wishing I could be one of them. Although I never wanted to stop having adventures, I did want to have a place to call home. That chance was gone, however, and I had to keep pushing forward.

But at least I had Zach.

He was moving a bit slower still, but he seemed a lot better than when he woke up. He had his ginger hair pulled back in a bun, and his beard was a bit scruffier than what he preferred. We definitely needed a nice place to stay and clean up.

We grabbed our horses, which were kept close to our hotel, although their conditions were a lot nicer than ours. I realized I should have just slept out here as there appeared to be fewer bugs and the water they had was clear. We cared for them more than we cared for ourselves as it wasn't their fault that their owners were Kausian.

I tipped the horse-stall owner a few extra coins, and we made our way through the city. I kept an eye out for anyone who might look for us after the stunt we pulled last night—mainly Silurians. So far, it was still early and there weren't that many people out and about. Silurians preferred nighttime anyway as they could see in the dark. I was thankful for this since I really didn't want to cause another shoot-out. We were always blamed for things that weren't technically our fault, so I didn't want to cause another scene.

We rode our horses through the dirt-and-stone streets and came upon the border of the city. They would check our ID on the way out and make sure we didn't have any warrants or bills we still needed to pay. Typically it was easier to leave than it was to enter, as beyond the walls was all wilderness, whether it be forest, mountain, or desert, and they didn't care if you went out to die— as long as you didn't have money owed anywhere, of course. Most people lived inside cities and towns, if not close to them and still within the zones. It was very rare to live by oneself, not under protection of any zone.

Because then bandits could come along and burn your house down, and no one would do a thing about it.

Five Lyrans stood at the border, checking the few people trying to leave this early. They were barely glancing at the IDs and waving people through. This would be easy, or at least I hoped.

There was already a lengthy line of people entering, meaning a lot of the focus was on making sure no one was a fugitive before they were free to roam the city. Lucky for us, wanted ads didn't make it far throughout the different zones and, unless you pissed off the wrong people, were likely to go off anyone's radar within a few weeks.

The Lyran took our IDs, glanced at them, and then did a double take.

I whispered, "Shit."

Taking out his gun, he aimed it at us. "Elvira Ryder and Zachariah Richards, you're under arrest for the killing of three Silurians."

I grasped the sand I kept in a bag within arm's reach for such an occasion and threw it in the eyes of the Lyran. He roared, cursing and yelling for backup. And grabbed his gun.

"Run!" I yelled at Zach.

He kicked his horse, and we bolted out of the zone and into the forest. They fired shots after us, but thank the gods they did not hit us or our horses as we made it to the tree line. Our horses were some of the finest, and we kept them healthy so we could run away like this.

After at least half an hour of high-tailing it through the brush, just to make sure they didn't follow after, I slowed down my horse Kevin and stopped at a little lake that appeared in the middle of the wilderness. I dropped down beside Kevin and let him get the water he needed. Zach did the same with Char.

"What was that? We didn't kill those Silurians." Zach reached down and splashed water on his face.

I took a drink of water from our canteen. "I have no idea. We used tranks."

"You know we can't go back to that zone for a while, don't you? How are we going to get the info about Cor now?"

I shook my head. "I don't know. We will figure out something. We can always send him a telegram or call. Let him know what happened."

"Yeah, like that will work."

It was my turn to dunk my face in the water. The second sun was making its way up on the horizon, and I was sweating already. We had little choice now. Someone had lied to the authorities. It could have been for a few different reasons, one including just wanting to cause us trouble because we were Kausian, or someone received word about the assassination and they didn't want us to go through with it.

We would have to be on our guard, even more so than normal.

CHAPTER VII

<u>Zach</u>

Well, it didn't seem like anyone followed us out into the woods.

Two days had passed, and we hadn't run into a single person or wild animal yet. I was surprised as we usually had one or two run-ins when we traveled. I didn't want to deal with bandits again, and I felt bad having to defend against wolves or other creatures. We had guns and knives and no hesitation to kill if need be.

Although we figured no one from the Lyran Zone

followed us, we had kept an eye out for anything strange. We didn't want to push our horses too much on the first day of travel, so we slowed down a bit and stayed alert. Now we were coming to our third setting of the suns and would have to stop for the night.

"Shouldn't we stop pretty soon? Suns are going down and I'm tired," I stated as I patted Char. Ellie was in the lead, as usual. I would just get us lost.

"I want to get over these two hills. Should be there in about an hour or so," she called back from on top of her horse, Kevin.

I sighed. I remembered this path she discovered before, and there would be a cave up ahead. I didn't particularly like caves. They creeped me out, and I swore I always heard something coming from them. And Ellie never believed me.

We couldn't exactly stay on the roads since there were sometimes peacemakers and such and because Ellie swore this way was faster. It seemed like it was as long as we didn't get attacked by a bear or a cougar or worse…

At least we could transform into something that scared the beasts away if need be, but trying to go after our horses afterward was a whole different matter. So typically we fought them off without using our shifter powers. It was easier in the long run.

"Are we there yet?" I sarcastically whined.

Ellie shot me a look from over her shoulder. She hated it when I asked that, so I tended to ask it often when we traveled, which was frequently.

"I swear to the gods, Zachariah Richards, if you ask me that one more time, I'll run a bullet through your pretty red head."

I laughed. "You wouldn't shoot me. You don't think I'm worth the price of the bullet."

Nodding, she added, "You're right. I would just grab a stick and bash your head open instead."

She had me there as I doubted she was kidding.

Taking a deep breath, I took note of the clean, woodsy air. I loved being outdoors like this and wished we could stay out here forever. We tried at one point, but that didn't end so well. There were a lot of bandits who could find us if we stayed still, which was always a downer. They liked to loot things, start fires, and try to kill whomever they came across. Luckily Ellie was a marvelous shot, but bullets were expensive, and even though it was self-defense and not in any zone, if any officers found out, they might try to arrest us—which was stupid because we were getting rid of the bandits for them. I had a feeling it was because we were Kausian rather than that we did something wrong. They used any excuse to put us behind bars.

So in general we caused havoc. It was what they expected of us.

Turning up toward the sky, I closed my eyes. Although both suns were an equal distance from the world currently, which made it one of the two hottest times of the year, the heat felt pleasant. We Kausians used to live in the middle of the desert on this planet, so heat was nothing new to us, especially up north where there were trees and lakes and whatnot. Most of the locals in these parts complained this time of year, but if they really wanted to complain about something, then they should travel to the city of Kaus, or what's left of it anyway.

There was a reason we shifted—to become a race that could endure the heat in the summers and a race to endure the harsh winters. Yeah, we had both crappy winters and summers. But the in-between was perfect for our normal body type, and shifting kept us going for the rest. Sounds horrible, yes, but it was home.

"Are we there yet?"

I felt something hit me straight in the forehead. Opening my eyes, I found Ellie with a few acorns in her hand.

"Next one will be in your eye, and you will be wearing a patch for the rest of your days."

I held up my hands. "Calm down. I'm just teasing. I swear I won't ask again. But really, we have been traveling for quite some time. You sure we are going to make it to the Human Zone in time?"

She shrugged. "I think so. We have traveled this way before and made it in about six days, give or take a day. As long as the human hasn't left, we should be fine."

"Then we will find the man called Gabriel, assassinate him, and take a nice hot bath." I grinned.

She rolled her eyes. "Something like that, yes. The Human Zone definitely has the most relaxing baths. But we need to get back to get our info."

"But we also need baths. Byron can wait the extra hour we take to get baths. Besides, we need to figure out how to get back to the Lyran Zone, if not just send someone in for us. Or call him."

Ellie shook her head. "I don't trust anyone to go in for us—not with the information he is carrying. Phone call might be fine, but then I can't see his face to tell if he is lying or not."

She had a point. There wasn't one person we could trust. They would see we were Kausian and just use us. Probably just take our money and disappear. That's what they all did. We were lucky that we ever got paid. Ellie was smart though and demanded half up front and the rest once the job was finished. It was why she asked for bullets, knowing that he might not actually have anything on Cor and because we needed bullets.

"So want to play a game?" I asked.

Ellie sighed. "What game do you suggest?"

I shrugged. "I don't know. How about I spy?"

"Fine. You can go first."

I glanced around at the surrounding forest. "I spy something… green."

She gave me her signature look and let out a breath. "Is it a plant?"

"But which plant?"

She let her head drop. "Oh my gods, I don't know." She pointed with her finger. "That one?"

"Nope! Guess again!"

"Zach… Do I have to?"

I nodded. "Of course. What else are we going to do for the next few days?"

"I don't know, maybe enjoy the peace and quiet that is nature?"

Glancing around, I realized she had a point. The nature here was beautiful, the sky was clear, and the scent of the foliage was sweet and innocent. Even the birds were chirping. I watched as a butterfly fluttered past us. It seemed like there were a lot of butterflies this summer—it was almost eerie in a way as it was so wonderful that it didn't seem real.

"Fine. I'll just sing us a song!" I smiled and took in a deep breath. "His roar echoes through the forest. His eyes pierce through the night. Searching for his long-lost master, who will set things right!"

"Please stop, I beg of you!" She might have been protesting, but I could see the smirk on her lips.

"It's the creature who protects this planet, one that can never leave. He gave his oath to his master, and now it's been centuries of…" I paused, biting my bottom lip. "What was the last word?"

"If he had to deal with you, it was probably centuries of agony."

"That's rude. I was just trying to entertain you."

She let out a breath. "I know, Zach. Sorry, it's just…" She clutched her shirt where I knew the ring that Cor had given her hung. "I want all this to be over with. Then I can finally feel ready to move on."

I doubted she would—she was still holding on to that ring, after all. Even if she killed him—which, again, I highly doubted—it wouldn't change anything. Our home would still be gone, and our backs would still have been stabbed. Revenge was a dangerous thing, but all I could do at this point was support Ellie until she figured out what she really wanted in life.

"Where did you find that song anyway?" Ellie changed the subject. I had almost forgotten I had been singing.

I had to think. Where had I heard it from? "Maybe it was in a book I read when we were teens. Some science fiction or fantasy book? I can't remember."

She chuckled. "I didn't know you read books, Zach. Who would have thought."

"I used to always read! You know that!"

"I was just teasing, Zach. I know you love to read. If it weren't for the fact that books are heavy, I would let you have all the books you want."

I grinned. "Why, thank you. I dream one day to own a library and let anyone use it. More people need to read, you know. Books teach us how to live and think."

"A library, huh? And what should I aspire to have?" She seemed genuinely curious. I thought about it for a moment.

"I dunno, some gross whiskey bar? Or a shooting range?"

"Or maybe both?"

"Yeah, that would end well."

Laughing, we headed forward toward the Human Zone, hoping that the job would be successful and we could find Cor once and for all. It was all we wanted— it was all we could want at this point.

There was nothing left for us—most everyone else was murdered in the attack. We knew of a few other Kausians around, but they laid low, trying not to be noticed. It was why most didn't welcome Ellie and me. We were a bit too noticeable. We had performed many, many crimes and had lots of outstanding bounties and warrants on our heads.

Luckily, no zone was organized enough to catch us. Yet.

But once all this was over, which honestly could be within the week, then we would be on our way, mission completed, and live in this wilderness. Hopefully this time we wouldn't get ambushed. We would have to find somewhere far away from everything.

Then the two of us could live our lives.

CHAPTER VIII

<u>Cor</u>

I didn't know if the looks I got for wearing sunglasses were better than the looks I got for the color of my eyes.

At least all the girls still smiled at me. I ran my fingers through my white-blond hair and gave them a smile. The three human women who were staring giggled and turned red. I tapped my credit pass on the scanner, and it glowed green as the entrance to the spaceport opened. Ignoring the stares from others, I stuffed my hands in my pockets and kept on walking. Yeah, the looks they gave me when they realized I was a Kausian were a lot worse—these were just disapproving sneers from rich folk who thought I was a stupid human. If I took my glasses off, there would be looks of pure hatred and resentment.

And then some asshole would try to assault me.

I knew all this from experience, of course. I had lost count of how many times I had gotten into fights, most of which I hadn't started, but I sure as hell ended. Most of the guys that attacked me thought since they outnumbered me, they would win. Many had learned how wrong they truly were. Gabe, on the other hand, couldn't handle himself in a fight, which was why I always had to protect him first. He was lucky I was so skilled at fighting. I had saved his ass more than once as there were people in the society that wanted him dead.

Which was why I was heading up to make sure there were no traps waiting for him.

It was easier to deal with traps when he wasn't around as I didn't have to try to protect him. It meant, however, that he was all alone where he was. So far, no one had tried anything, but that didn't mean they wouldn't. I took a deep breath and let it out slowly. I didn't need to worry—he had a gun and wasn't that bad in a fight if need be. I just had to keep telling myself that.

Once I was inside the spaceport, I made my way toward the only transport this place had as there was only one location a person could visit in space, and that was the moon Zynon. The area was busy, and I was careful not to accidentally kick a kid that paid no mind to others as they zoomed in every direction. I should have tried to get a seat in business class, but I didn't want to deal with all the glares and murmurs. Then again, I also didn't want to deal with these kids. Too late now.

I stepped onto the stairs that lead up to the multipassenger KR67 Transporter along with what appeared to be two hundred other passengers. I didn't know it was possible for this many people to afford to visit Zynon. My guess was that a lot of them were on a tour package as half the moon was a big campy theme park.

And the other half, well, that's where the real fun was.

The other half of Zynon was for the rich and elite of all the zones, excluding Kaus of course, at least when it was a zone. Shady business deals, assassinations, drugs, you name it, and it was there. It was like all the shady parts of the human zones, but I would never say that to these folks. No, they were above those types of folk. That was total bullshit. They were the same except they dressed nicer.

At check-in, I handed in my two 5Y743 revolvers as there were no guns allowed on the ship, but you could check them in at a designated kiosk to retrieve them once we were in Zynon. It was a pain as the line would be long once we arrived at our destination, but it was well worth dealing with the fuss to stay armed within the city. I grabbed my ticket and stuffed it in a zipped pocket. There was no way I would lose it. Even if I had weapons stashed at the hotel on Zynon, I didn't want to set foot on the moon without one.

Finding my way through the transporter, I weaved around common folk of all species, wanting to find the quietest spot imaginable. I didn't particularly enjoy being on machines like this, but since it was the only way to the city, it was a must. Usually I had Gabe to distract me from the sickness that developed in my stomach, but this time I was alone.

Which made me worry even more.

I was sure there would be an assassination attempt on his life as he had no royal or elite status. He managed to gain entry into the society by other means. Many people did not like that fact, and since he was going to be voted into the society this week, it was an even bigger possibility.

However, I didn't know if the attempt would be in Zynon or back in the Human Zone. Gabe said he could handle things in the Human Zone, and I should sweep the place up on Zynon to check for anyone suspicious planning something. I didn't disagree, clearly, since I was heading there now, but I still worried. I just couldn't wait until this was over and I could have him in my arms again.

Venturing through the different large, warehouse-size rooms, I found a little shadowed corner I could sit in for the six-hour ride. I rested my head against the wall and watched as the remaining passengers gathered on board. Most of them were human, as we were departing the Human Zone, but there were also quite a few Silurians, which I found odd. I narrowed my eyes as I inspected them. They didn't seem like they were up to anything as they remained in groups and glared at anyone who came near. Usually they stayed away from the Human

Zone as humans weren't to their liking. I would monitor them and make sure I stayed out of their sight. They hated Kausians with a passion. I would know after everything that had happened.

Letting out a breath, I watched as a Lyran cub ran around playing with a toy model of the transporter. He kept crashing it into things, making me even more motion sick. I didn't understand how all the other species were fine with these types of craft. It wasn't natural—no machine was natural. I preferred a safe, faithful horse any day. Or cattle with a wagon even. No, Kausians and machines didn't mix. It was a universal thing as I didn't remember any of my friends liking machines either.

My heart felt as if it had slipped down into my stomach, not helping my nausea. Why I kept tormenting myself by thinking about my past I didn't know. What was done was done, and I couldn't change that. I was a teenager. I didn't know better.

I smacked my head back on the wall purposefully. I had known better. I was just stupid.

Clutching the ring in my pocket, I thought back to the woman I would have given everything for—the person I was willing to go above and beyond just to see smile.

I knew everything that transpired was my fault and that she would never want to see my face ever again. But I would right my wrongs though. No matter what it took. Then maybe I could find her...

Bringing my attention back to the present, I could smell the faint stench of the engines as they were getting ready to fly up into the sky combined with the aroma of fried chicken and sausage. My stomach didn't know if it should be more upset or hungry as I had skipped breakfast. Maybe it wouldn't be such an awful idea to grab something to eat to kill time.

As I stood up, the transporter moved. I held my hand to my mouth. I would not get sick. I. Would. Not. Get. Sick. Running to the trash can, I emptied any contents my stomach had from the night before. It was just bile. I could feel eyes on me as the other passengers stared. Wiping my mouth, I turned to find a group of Silurians eyeing me. Few other species got sick, other than Kausians and humans. I was lucky I looked like a human; otherwise, it would have been very suspicious. I was, however, wearing sunglasses, so that wasn't helping my case.

I hurried toward the concession stands in the other section of the ship. As I exited the seating section, I found myself in almost a bizarre-looking place. Dozens upon dozens of tents and tables were set up with food, knickknacks, clothing, books, art—you name it, it was there. It was like what you would see in a city except it was on this transporter. I never understood why they had so many shops on the ship as there were plenty of shops in Zynon, but nevertheless, they apparently were doing well as everyone crowded there to pass the time. A group of Sirians gathered around a table of seashells, which made no sense to me as they literally lived in the sea. Could they not find somewhere they lived that wasn't overpriced? Maybe it was just my temper since they blocked the entire section and I wanted to get by and buy something to eat.

"Excuse me," I said as I tried to make my way through. They didn't move. I rolled my eyes.

"Excuse me," I repeated a little more loudly.

The elderly Sirian stared at me as if I was being rude. I turned and went all the way around to the next row. I hated people like that, not to mention it was hurting the sales of tables nearby as no one could get to them.

I made my way through the crowd to the booth that smelled of fried chicken. I noticed that there were a lot of children on this transporter. I supposed it was

what I would have done without your help."

I shrugged. "It was nothing. Now get going before they change their minds."

He nodded quickly, ran around me, and disappeared a few moments later.

I whispered to myself, "Crimes should always be punished, huh? Who am I kidding?"

Rubbing the back of my neck, I strolled over to my seat to find my chicken bucket gone.

"Fuck!"

CHAPTER IX

Gabe

Stay in the hotel room, he says. Don't go outside, he says.

As if.

Cor was a little too overprotective sometimes. It wasn't as if I were going to be shot dead if I walked out in the street or went down and played some poker. No, it was more likely I would be assassinated if I lingered in my room as there wouldn't be anyone around to stop the killer. If I remained in a crowd, however, then I would be safe.

And maybe I could find someone to keep me company tonight to be extra cautious. Or cause them to be murdered too. It could go either way.

I knew I shouldn't be so relaxed about it, but after nineteen years of people either attempting to kill me or threatening to kill me, I had gone a bit numb. Cor acts like he was the one always protecting me, as if I hadn't been taking care of myself on my own for a few years. Besides, most of the people trying to kill us had been after him originally, and he wasn't here, so I should be fine.

Other than that man knowing possibly where I was at the moment.

But who in the world knew where he was? He traveled a lot, so he could be miles away and would have had to send people all the way here. The odds of that were slim. No, more than likely he would send someone up in Zynon to do his bidding. Lucky for me, Cor was already on that.

So I had nothing to fear.

And therefore, I could go have a pleasant stroll in town. Grabbing my top hat and cane, I headed down the stairs from my hotel room and onto the streets.

We—before Cor left at least—were currently residing in Arcadia, the town on the edge of the capital in the Human Zone. The Human Zone itself is made up of fifteen thousand square miles, fifty if one counted all the way to what were supposed to be the borders. Really, it was run by bandits, and anything not within the walls of the Human Zone was fair game with no rules or regulations. I did not like venturing out there and typically took the train. The train was so much more relaxing.

But Arcadia was near the entrance to the zone, and many people used the town to trade goods they had picked up from other zones or even in the wilderness if they were crafty and had excellent survival skills. I was always surprised to hear how many could make it out there and less shocked by how many bodies were reported on a day-to-day basis. And those were the ones that were found.

The street was covered in dirt and cobble, and I took care not to get run over by a carriage or horse. I could easily hail a taxi and sit in comfort as I watched the buildings pass by, but today I wanted to venture out and see if there were any nice things I could pick up for myself or Cor before heading up to Zynon the next day.

Besides, it was a pleasant summer day, and the second sun hadn't quite risen over the mountains. I glanced up. There were a couple of stray clouds, but otherwise, it was the perfect day. I was sure it would become hotter by the time afternoon came around, but I could always cool off in the ocean if my skin dried out a little too much.

Although I was in the Human Zone, there were plenty of other races wandering around, looking for things to buy or sell. There weren't many Silurians, mainly because it was still before noon and they didn't care for mornings. It was a wonder they weren't like the Pleiadeans, who created a haven for only them. I supposed it was because then they couldn't cause trouble and show how strong they were.

The smell of bread and baked goods stopped me in my tracks. I turned to find a bakery across the street. Making sure there wasn't any traffic coming, I hurried to the other side and stepped inside the small shop.

My mouth dropped in quick astonishment as I drooled over the stacks of pastries and every type of bread imaginable. I couldn't believe I hadn't come to this place before as Cor and I loved any sort of good food. When we got back, I would have to bring him here.

There was an elderly couple buying a bag of breads at the front, but otherwise, it was vacant. I wasn't sure how it could be so empty when there was so much to purchase and because the smell drew you in as you walked by.

The most troublesome part of all this was that I would have to figure out what I wanted to buy. I didn't have Cor here to purchase a dozen with and then share them all. I could eat three but would have a stomach ache later. It was worth it though.

The elderly couple finished up what they were buying and left the shop, leaving me as the only customer. The shopkeeper turned to me and smiled.

"Is there anything you need help with?"

She had dark hair that was pulled back in a bun and a beautiful white smile that contrasted her skin. She had on a plaid dress and appeared young enough to be the daughter or just a helper of this shop. More than likely, she wasn't the one doing the actual baking.

"I can't decide on what to buy. There are so many flavors."

She nodded. "I agree. I get allowed one a day as part of my pay, and I can never decide. Well, what are your favorite types of fruit? Or do you prefer cheese or plain bread?"

"Yes," I answered with a quick smirk. "Meaning I love it all."

"Well, then I will tell you my favorites. First off, you can never go wrong with a cheese danish, and the cheese danishes here are like no other."

"I will take one of those then. What other two should I get?"

She bit her lip. "If you want to have a bit of a variety, I would say get a regular or chocolate one and a fruit one. The seasonal right now is a peach cardamom donut. And one can never go wrong with peaches, and the cardamom is just light enough where it accents the peach instead of overpowers it. And it's not overly sweet either."

"That sounds delightful. I will take that and… yeah, let's go with the chocolate. Those all sounds great."

The girl grinned widely. "I will get that all in a bag for you. That will be ten copper."

I reached into my pocket and grabbed some coins. Although in the fancier areas, one's card was used to exchange currency, in small places like this, coins still existed. It was easier that way, as many didn't trust the government to make sure the cash hadn't been tampered with, not to mention there had been cases of hacking. Using coins made businesses like this feel safe.

Giving her an extra two copper, I left with my pastries in hand and munched on the peach donut as I ventured farther down the road. She wasn't joking—this was the best donut I had ever had. It was sweet and flavorful, not too much where it ruined the delicate flavoring. I glanced down at it. I could eat a hundred of these things. Someone could easily poison me with one of these, and I honestly wouldn't care.

Deciding to save the two for a little later, I pressed forward. More and more carriages were appearing in the street as people got up and ready for work. Even though I stayed up late most nights, I took delight in mornings. Cor, on the other hand, was not a morning person. He was bitchy, to say the least. None of the patrons he slept with got to witness it as he always came back to the bedroom before the sun was up. Then I got to deal with Morning Cor. It was not fair.

Even so, I missed him already, grumpiness and all.

I caught sight of one of my favorite stores—the hat store. One could never have too many hats—at least that was what I believed. I beelined it straight there, making sure my hands were clean so I didn't damage any of the hats I knew I was going to touch. As I entered, the hatter nodded to me.

"Mr. Pickett, back so soon?"

The hatter, Charles, was a tall human man with lengthy arms and legs to the point where he had to duck going in and out his own doorway.

"What can I say? I love your hats."

He made a sound that was halfway between a grunt and a chuckle. "Well, help yourself. Let me know if you need anything."

I nodded and peered around the shop. He really did make the best hats. Where I grew up, no one cared for hats, mainly because they weren't helpful while swimming. Perhaps I was rebelling against my upbringing was why I liked hats. Or perhaps it was because everyone in the society wore them and I wanted to fit in. Either way, the more I shopped around, the more I found that each hat was unique to the hatter.

Stopping in front of a green velvet top hat, I picked it up to try on. It felt as if it fit perfectly. I stepped in front of the mirror the shop had, and sure enough, I loved it. The green made my eyes a little lighter, which I liked. I didn't want to be recognized for what I really was.

"Looks good on you." Charles got up from his chair, careful not to hit his head on some of the lower beams. "Tell you what. I will give you ten percent off since you have been such a loyal customer."

I smiled. "You are too kind. I will take it. Just don't tell my partner."

Charles went back behind his table and began writing some numbers down. "Speaking of which, where is Cor?"

"He headed up to Zynon without me. I will be seeing him tomorrow though, and I know he's going to be jealous of this hat."

"I'm sure he will. That will be sixty copper."

I gave the man the copper coins and a couple extra for being kind. As I headed back onto the street, I took a bite of the cheese danish this time. I closed my eyes as it melted in my mouth. This was paradise. I wished I could spend every day like this. But I knew that wasn't possible—not when so many wanted both Cor and me dead.

Other than being a Kausian, I wasn't sure why Cor seemed to always be looking over his shoulder. It wasn't as if I didn't keep secrets from him, so I never bothered finding out the truth. He would tell me when he wanted to. Just like I would tell him the truth about who I really was.

I finished the danish and headed back toward the parlor and hotel. I needed to put together the perfect outfit to go with this hat, and then tonight I would find me someone to spend the night with, just to be on the safe side.

CHAPTER X

<u>Ellie</u>

The week passed and there were no more hiccups, which surprised both of us. We even got through the checkpoint with no problems. I didn't think that there was anywhere left where we weren't on some wanted list or another. After this mission, however, we would be as we were about to assassinate a man named Gabriel Pickett.

Leading the horses to find a stall, we looked for the nicest place that we could afford. Both Kevin and Char were tired and deserved all the pampering possible. We also had the cash to do so.

We arrived around lunchtime, which was perfect because I wanted real food instead of the dried protein and nutrition bars we had been gnawing on for the past week. But first thing was first—we had to put our horses somewhere to rest. We found a place, and I paid the owner a bit more than he was asking—something I did to make sure they didn't mess with our horses because we were Kausian.

"We may need to leave town in a hurry." I nudged Zach with my elbow. "This man here has a wife who is about to go to labor, and we might have to book it back home. However, this short business couldn't wait, so here we are."

The human male, who was elderly with shaggy white hair and beard, looked us over with his crystal-blue eyes. He pulled out his pipe and let out a breath. "I didn't know your kind even had anywhere to call home."

My lips curled into a smile. It wasn't a cheerful smile, of course, but a smile you made when that was all you had left from the past. "Lucky for us, we found a house in the wastelands. So please get our horses fed, watered, and cleaned."

I flipped my coat back so he could see my gun. His eyes lingered on it for a moment, and he nodded. I grinned, knowing he caught my drift.

Turning on my heel, I left the man standing there before I could break that pipe of his in his mouth with my fist. Zach followed quickly behind but said nothing.

Because that fellow was right—we didn't have a home.

Which brought us back to the task at hand: find Gabriel Pickett, kill him, and we could get intel on where exactly Cor was. It had been three years, and now it could be only a few days more when I would get to find him and take out my revenge. He was good at hiding, which was impressive because we were good at grabbing attention no matter where we were. People noticed when Kausians stepped into a district, and the fact Cor could go unnoticed was rather troublesome.

But now we had a lead, and all we had to do was kill some punk.

Granted, it was immoral to kill someone who probably didn't deserve it, but it was also immoral to let your entire nation be destroyed. Cor needed to pay for what he did, and this guy was in the way of that. If we didn't kill him, someone else would. That was just the way it was in this world, so I might as well get something out of it.

"So the intel said he would be at the parlor hotel near the pier. He gambles a bunch, then drinks and gets hammered," Zach added as he flipped through the papers one last time.

"Good, that makes our job easier. He won't put up much of a fight if he is wasted."

"That's what I was thinking. Once he is drunk, you could seduce him, and then I'll follow you two to his room, and then we kill them. We can leave straightaway before anyone finds the body."

I nodded. "That sounds like a good plan, except I smell and don't have clothes that are very suitable for seducing someone."

"Didn't Bryce or whatever his name was give us some credits up front? We can buy you a dress and perhaps something fancy for me and then go to the bath house real quick. The night is young, is it not? We have plenty of time."

I frowned. He had a point. There was no way I could seduce him with what I was wearing. But then again, we didn't have to go about it in this fashion. Except it was the easiest. From what we knew about the human, he seemed the type to be trusting and wouldn't question a woman wanting to go to bed with him.

Sighing, I gave in. "Fine, we will do it your way."

It took about four hours for us to get lunch and then find a dress that fit. Zach had to try on three different suits for some odd reason, and then we really needed to bathe and do my hair. I didn't have makeup, so that was out of the question. A woman at the bath offered me some of hers, but I declined. Who knew what kind of diseases you could acquire when using someone else's lipstick?

I stepped out of the changing room in a red dress with black ruffles and sleeves. I did not like wearing this at all. I felt like some of the prostitutes who stayed at the hotels, offering men and women services all night long. I didn't consider that line of work wrong or anything, but it just wasn't what I wanted to do.

"Zach... I don't think this is a good idea..."

He was wearing the all-black suit he picked out, which made him look more like an assassin, but I didn't say that. He looked pretty good in black. Zach stepped up to me and grabbed my hands. "You look so beautiful! All the men will be staring at you tonight."

I rolled my eyes. "I don't want all the men looking at me like that. I just want to do my job."

"You don't enjoy dressing feminine, do you?"

"Nope."

He sighed. "Well, you look good and definitely will catch his eye."

"The only problem is…" I pointed at my eyes. "These eyes are a dead giveaway for what we are. Do you think he'll care?"

Zach shrugged. "Only one way to find out. Besides, I've heard that the very few Kausians who are still alive are actually making it as prostitutes since they can shift into any species. Maybe he'll think you're one of them."

I punched him in the arm for good measure and we left the bathhouse. The parlor hotel wasn't far and would only take a few minutes to walk.

"We probably don't want to enter together as it would give him the wrong idea. Perhaps you come in a few minutes after me? Also, you should wear your sunglasses. Two Kausians in a building might look a little suspicious as well."

He nodded. "Got it."

"The plan is to get him drunk, have him take me to his room, then I'll step out on the patio, motion to you so you see what room he's in, then I'll keep the balcony unlocked, and we murder the poor bastard before anyone knows what's up."

"Sounds like a plan."

"Can you climb up in that outfit? Looks a little restrictive in some areas."

Zach gave me a look as he stopped, and I went on toward the entrance of the parlor, laughing to myself.

The parlor was huge—larger than any other I had ever seen. I gaped at the chandeliers that hung down from the tall ceiling. How much money did that cost? And where did they even find crystals that large? We had nothing like that in Kaus—even the richer Kausians lived about the equivalent of a middle-class human. Then the rest of us barely got by, but we had each other and there was a sense of community. I couldn't say we had ever seen a community that looked out for one another anywhere else like we Kausians did.

The more I peered around, the more I realized everything was blue. I was glad I didn't pick a blue dress or else everyone would think I worked here. I noted where the bar was and would try to draw Gabriel to it. Then we could have a couple of drinks, I could lead him up to his hotel room, and then we could assassinate him. Easy peasy.

Stepping forward, I scanned for any signs of Gabriel. Since he appeared very much like a human, it was going to take me a bit to find. I started weaving through the different game tables that had roulette, poker, faro, three-card monte, and hazard, just to name a few. As I glanced at all the men at the tables, I noticed the mark wearing an obnoxious green hat and suit.

He was sitting at a blackjack table, which was a card game that I enjoyed playing since I was quite good—or lucky, according to Zach. He just didn't understand the game well enough.

I took a seat a few chairs from Green Hat and gave the dealer a wad of cash to transfer into chips. The man did just that, and I was now in the game.

The dealer handed out a card to each of us and flipped his own face up. I peeked at my card. It was a seven, which wasn't the best card to have starting off.

Dealing out the rest of the cards, the male dealer gave me a four, which made eleven. Maybe my luck wasn't bad after all. The person sitting next to me went first but passed.

"Hit me," I said with a smile. I glanced over at Gabriel, but he seemed too interested in his own cards. I expected more people to be around him, but he was alone that night. Lucky me.

The dealer placed down a jack, and I grinned. "I will stay."

The two other players before Gabriel played, one of them going over twenty-one and the other stayed after two more cards, but he only had a nineteen. I watched Gabriel stare at his cards with a perplexed look on his face, as if he didn't know what to do.

"Hit me," he finally said. It was a four. And he also had twenty-one. He grinned. "I will stay."

The dealer went and dealt himself over twenty-one, which meant the dealer had to pay both of us out and the man that had under twenty-one. I glanced over at Gabriel and gave him a wink.

"Well, it seems we are both lucky tonight," I said. I knew I sucked at this, but men never seemed to care.

"And I don't even have my lucky charm with me. It's a surprise I won at all," he commented.

The comment took me back. Was he in a relationship? If so, was this going to work? Well, only one way to find out. "Perhaps I could be your lucky

while.

"So are you busy later tonight?" Gabriel asked as he stroked my hand. "I bet you could show a man a good time."

I gulped. I mean, maybe? I didn't know, as I had never slept with a man—or woman, if I were honest— so I couldn't really say. But it wasn't like I would actually sleep with him, since I was going to kill him first, so I took his hand and gave it a kiss. "Oh, I can show you things that will blow your mind." With a gun, actually. I tried not to smile at my joke.

Gabriel grinned. "I thought so. I saw your drink, and I just could tell."

For the last time, the type of drink one had did not entail someone's sexuality! But I didn't say that to him. I wanted him to believe I was interested so I could figure out which room he was in and let Ellie know. I glanced over at Ellie again and found her, hand on hip, peeved at the situation. She would now have to go around back and climb up to the balcony. In that dress.

This night kept getting better and better.

"What is your name?"

I hesitated. I didn't want to give him my real name, of course, but all my fake names I usually went with escaped me. "It's Bartholomew. The third." I didn't know why I added the third, but it just seemed to go with the name. Same for Char.

"Well, that name is a mouthful. I hope the rest of you is as well," he added with a bit of a smirk. I felt my cheeks turn red, which they did easily after a drink.

I didn't know what to do next. I hadn't hit on anyone, well, ever. It was just never on my agenda, as Ellie and I had been on the road, running away or looking for work for three years. I squeaked. "How about I show you now?"

His eyes widened a little, and then he smiled. "Well, you get to the point quickly. Let me finish up my business with this lady, and then we can be on our way."

I wondered to what business he would have with Ellie since he left her to talk to me. I couldn't quite hear their conversation from where I stood, and I didn't want to seem like I was trying to eavesdrop, so I didn't get any closer. But by the look on Ellie's face, she didn't appreciate what he was saying.

I was so going to hold this over her after.

She looked like she wanted to kill him right then and there but couldn't as then there would be witnesses. She folded her arms in front of herself, as she usually did when she didn't want to do something drastic. I saw her glance my way, and I simply smiled. This made her cheeks get even more red.

After they were done talking, Ellie walked away, and Gabriel looked sort of perplexed and a little embarrassed. What in the world could they have discussed?

Gabriel grabbed his coat and came back over to where I was waiting.

"What was that about?" I asked, which wasn't odd for someone to ask, especially if they supposedly were going to have a fling. I could have been wondering due to it becoming a three-way or something.

"Oh, I thought she was looking for work and was going to help, but apparently there was some miscommunication. I suppose I should be double-checking with you as well. Is this just a one-night stand, or do I need to pay you?"

I was taken back. "Excuse me?"

He shook his head. "I did it again. I'm sorry. I noticed that you and she were both from Kaus. Generally, in the parts I frequent, your kind are prostitutes. I offered to find her some men for the night, and apparently she was just interested in me. I should have figured… But I didn't think you were as you didn't come on to me, but now with this misunderstanding, I thought I would ask."

"How did you notice my eyes?" I inquired as they were well hidden behind the glasses. Even I couldn't tell in the mirror what color my eyes were.

He shrugged. "I know someone with eyes like yours, so I'm used to seeing them under different glasses. Most people can't tell, but I'm getting used to it. The two of us are an item, but we have an open relationship, so don't you worry."

Wait, this guy's in a relationship with a Kausian? That seemed very unlikely. I mean, what were the odds that he would be dating one of us, on top of being killed by two of us, to find the whereabouts of another one of us? This was getting confusing.

"Well, I'm not a prostitute. I'm just here for a good time."

Gabriel put his hand on my back and moved it down just above my butt. "Even better."

I held back a gulp. I was not used to a man being this handsy with me. Was this what women felt like? I did not envy them. Though, to be fair, I had come across quite a few handsy people. Usually it was a fist fight, not something like this.

"Do you know her?" Gabriel nodded the way Ellie had walked off.

I shook my head. "No. I'm actually only half, so there's not many Kausians like me. But then neither do humans nor any species for that matter."

"I thought your hair color was strange for a Kausian. Well, I love it. But now I'm more curious about what else I might love."

I gave him my most sexy grin, or at least what I figured was my sexy grin, and gestured toward the stairs that led to the hotel rooms. "Lead the way."

Gabriel wrapped his arm around my waist and started toward his room. His fingers traveled down a little farther than I wanted, but soon this all would be over. I just had to play the part, get in his room, go out on the balcony, and leave the door unlocked.

He traveled up to the fourth floor, which made me smile a little. Now Ellie would have to climb all the way up there. Was she going to change real quick, or was she going to scale the balconies in that dress? Damn, I wanted to watch if she picked the latter.

Men and women littered the hallway as we reached

the fourth floor. Most were men making out with women who might or might not have been prostitutes. Some women were making out with other women as well. And men with men. And a few groups.

I didn't know where to avert my eyes. They were everywhere.

Granted, Ellie and I had seen our fair share of things on the road, not to mention been invited for a few motel parties or could hear things through the walls, but we stayed out of it all. Neither of us were interested in that sort of thing, which worked out great for us as we could share a room without either of us wondering if the other wanted more. We made it clear we didn't. I didn't feel a need for relationships, and Ellie only wanted revenge against Cor, who incidentally was her ex.

Relationships seemed way too complicated to me.

Gabriel stopped in front of a door and then pushed me against it. Before I could let out an oomph, Gabriel's lips were on me. My eyes widened, and I was glad he had his own eyes closed or he would have noticed my surprise.

What do I do? What do I do?

I wrapped my arms around him like I wanted more, mimicking what he was doing. I didn't expect him to make a move so fast. Slowly, his hand traced down my chest and down lower to my pants.

Backing up, my voice squeaked. "How about we go to your room?"

He laughed. "To the point. I admire that."

No, actually, because I want to get your murder over with. Taking one more glance around, I realized it would be quite some time before someone would notice his murder. Thank the gods.

We entered his hotel room, which was rather plain. I honestly thought it would be full of gold and whatnot. Isn't that what those rich folks always had? Gold everything with silk and whatever was on the expensive list? This room just looked like a clearer hotel room than what Ellie and I had.

Gabriel shut the door behind me, and before I could do anything, he pushed me over to the bed and climbed on top of me.

Shit.

It felt like he had twenty pairs of hands as he was touching me all over and ripping my clothes off faster than I thought possible. I prayed he didn't rip a button because this was quite expensive. His lips were all over me fast, and I tried to push him back up. He took the hint and moved away.

"Are you not into this?"

No. "I am. It's just I find it way more romantic if we can have some time on the balcony and look over the city. It's kind of my kink." I knew it sounded stupid, but I was desperate. I didn't want to lose my virginity to someone I was about to kill. It didn't seem right.

He smiled. "To each their own, but I'll admit that I have the best view in the hotel. Come check it out."

I followed him over to the balcony, and he unlocked the door and pushed the doors open.

Okay, so the view was quite spectacular, I had to agree. You could see the city skyline and the ocean. In any normal situation, this would be something I would want to stare at for hours and enjoy the beauty, but normal didn't exist for us. I glanced down at the street and found Ellie throwing her arms up in exasperation. I grinned a little.

"Like what you see?" Gabriel asked as he stepped up behind me and wrapped his arms around my torso. He kissed my neck gently.

"Yeah." I gulped as I felt something hard forming against my ass. "I do. Is it okay if we stay out here just a bit longer? I doubt I'll be able to see a scene as nice as this."

"Sure thing. Take all the time you need."

I glanced down at Ellie again. Hurry, Ellie! Hurry!

CHAPTER XII

<u>Cor</u>

I stepped out of the KR67 Transporter and scanned my card on the reader so I could get my two 5Y743 revolvers back. I felt better once they were at my side again. There were some species that were stronger than me, after all, even if I transformed into one of them.

Once I was out of the spaceport, I found most of the passengers with their kids shuffling to the left, which led to the amusement park. I had to push through the crowd and head right, which was a task in and of itself.

Most who were going to the right were in the business class, which dropped them off straight at the front. It was another perk of traveling first class.

I had been to the amusement park twice, but I was pretty sure they still had a photo of me saying not to let me in again. It was a long time ago, and we didn't have money, and I wanted to take Ellie somewhere nice. It had been a lot of fun even when we got caught.

To the right, however, lay a part casino, part hotel, part meeting hall—all for the elite in each zone. Except Kaus, of course. Now I was technically part of this place by association. Oho ho, how the tables have turned. I would have laughed out loud, but I didn't need more eyes on me.

The structure was enormous, and even through the glass corridors that led to the two designated places, I could tell the casino was grander than the amusement park. Granted the amusement park's glass bubble was larger as it gave room in case of any accidents. And to supply all the families with fresh air, the casino's building took up as much area as the amusement park itself. It was crazy. One could definitely get absorbed in the maze of the elite.

Good thing I was excellent at getting around.

I would have to meet Gabe at the entrance of the casino tomorrow night, however, as he wasn't that great at directions. He'd gotten lost in the building every time we came up here, and I had to go find him. Luckily, he frequently gravitated toward a bar, so it was quick for me to spot him.

Taking another right and following the lit-up signs for the casino, I scanned my badge before the door. It lit green, and I was allowed in. A large human guard stood in front of the entrance, and as I was about to enter, he held out his hand.

"Not so fast. I would like to double-check your credentials."

I let out a sigh. This seemed to happen to me every single time. I had noticed before that he never stopped anyone else. Was it the glasses? Was it because I wasn't dressed properly? I was never brave enough to ask as I didn't want to be refused entry.

I handed him my card, and he scanned it. "You are associated with Gabriel Pickett. However, I don't see him with you."

"I was sent ahead as his security officer to make sure everything was safe for him."

The guard glanced over the card at me. "We are the

most secure facility in all the moon and the world below. There is no need for you to check anything out."

I shrugged. "Well, since last time someone tried to assassinate him, I beg to differ. There's a lot of people who don't quite like him. But either way, I belong here, as that card says."

The guard glared at me for a moment. "Fine. You're allowed to enter."

I snatched my card back. "Thank you."

I got out of there as quickly as I could before the guard changed his mind. I was not going to stay at the amusement park hotel again—not after what happened last time.

Heading straight to my—or Gabe's—suite, I decided it would be best to search the room for anything suspicious before checking the casino and meeting hall. Besides, I knew I needed to change into something a little more suitable for this company.

The elevators were, of course, on the entire other side of the casino. The casino was made up of six levels— the ground, which had a few different games and a buffet, then each level specialized in one game but had a plethora of tables. At each table, men and women were bidding with numbers that were hard for me to fathom. All the money used here in a day could feed the world below. But do they use it for that? Nope.

Most of these people undoubtedly possessed more wealth than all Kaus combined when it was still standing. Within Kaus, no one really used money as we didn't have the luxury of tourists and travelers. Most people helped each other out, and there was a trade system. Until the worst possible thing imaginable happened—the day I royally fucked up.

I shook my head, not wanting to bring back the memories. They weren't worth the trouble. The past was the past, and I needed to move forward. History couldn't be rewritten.

But I could find the truth behind it all and clear my name.

Instead of going through the casino, which was the fastest way to the elevators, I went through the corridor that circled around where everyone was playing roulette and craps. I didn't want to go through the crowd looking the way I did. The hallway was bad enough.

I made it to the elevator with no problems and pushed the button for the seventh floor. Two Lyrans got in with me and clicked the fourth floor, which was where most of the poker tables were at. I would be on that floor

guests of someone at the society. I could check the front
desk later if I wanted to, but I had a feeling it didn't
matter. More than one person wished Gabe dead, and I
would have to keep him alive until this induction
ceremony was over.

I pocketed the coins and gun I had found since they
wouldn't be using it anytime soon. I just needed to
figure out what I would do with the bodies. I was on the
seventh floor, which made disposing of them quite a
hassle.

As I stared at them, I got a knot in my stomach. What
if these two weren't the only ones who had been sent
after Gabe? What if someone figured he would stay
behind another day and sent some other bounty hunters
to the casino he frequented? I glanced over at the room
telephone. I had told him he could keep the bed warm
without me, and I didn't doubt he found someone to
sleep with, as he was good at that, so I didn't want to
bother him, but this feeling in the pit of my gut wasn't
going away. I just had to know.

I went over to the phone and dialed his room number.

CHAPTER XIII

Ellie

Son of a bitch.

Was I really supposed to climb up the side of this building to the fourth floor? I had done it before, but not in a dress and high heels.

Stupid Zach, seducing him instead of me.

Nowhere in the notes did it say that Gabe was gay. I didn't care one way or the other, but then I wouldn't have had to dress up and could have scaled this wall so much easier. I doubted I had time to change. This was all so stupid.

And he thought I was a prostitute. Ugh, Zach was never going to let me live this down. Then again, I was trying to seduce him in order to kill him.

There was only one thing to do now. I counted how many balconies there were. He was in the third room from the right. Okay, I could do this. I circled my head, got out any cracks that needed to be released, stretched my arms up and to the side a bit. I added a couple of calf and thigh stretches to be on the safe side. Taking a deep breath, I glanced back up at the balcony.

Who was I kidding?

I went back into the casino. There was no way I was going to climb quick enough for no one to notice. I was wearing bright red and stood out like a sore thumb. No, I would just pick the lock and go in the front.

I kept my eyes down, trying not to stand out, being a Kausian and all. This target had thought I was a prostitute, which meant that there might be a couple of Kausians around here who worked as one. I didn't want to be stopped by some men looking for a good time as I needed to go save Zach. And because I might stab a man who came near me wanting sex.

Trying to recall the last time Zach tried to seduce

someone, I was coming up blank. It wasn't his thing, and we rarely needed to seduce women or men who preferred men. We only did it this time because he was supposed to be a player and could get to his room and kill him before anyone noticed. Zach was probably in way over his head right now and freaking out.

I climbed up the stairs, careful not to twist my ankle. I hated heels so much. They were literally restraints for women, although I had found that I could do some damage with them if I kicked someone straight in the throat with one. Utterly ruined the shoes though.

It was still early in the evening, just after when most had dinner, so I was surprised by how many people were already heading to their room to have a good time. It was similar to all the other hotels Zach and I stayed at. This was why I preferred going out into the wilderness—there were fewer people to have to deal with and places I needed to avert my eyes from. There, of course, was the whole getting murdered in one's sleep though, but that also happened in hotels like these.

Like what I was about to do to Gabriel.

I made it to the fourth floor and started counting doors. He was the third to the right, if I recalled correctly, which I always did. I counted three from the right and tried the door. It was unlocked. I pulled the gun out of my bag and opened the door.

As quickly as I opened it, I shut it again, closing my eyes tight. I did not need to see an orgy right now. I tried to hold back the vomit. There were so many limbs —I wasn't even sure how many people were in that room. I looked back down the hallway.

Three from the right outside, three from the left on this side. Idiot.

Going down the hallway a little farther, I counted three from the left. I tried the door and found it was locked.

"Damn it, Zach," I sighed as I pulled out my lock picks. Glancing around, I found that none of the people in the hallway seemed to care that I was picking this lock since they were all making out with either one or maybe even two people. This was definitely not my scene. I wondered what kind of people who frequented this establishment would be like. Sexuality wasn't something I cared for as my mind was on revenge and that was all. Seemed like it would be a good time, though, in another life.

The door swung open, and I found Zach on the bed,

wide-eyed, as the target was on top of him, taking off his shirt. I quickly shut the door behind me and pointed the gun at him.

Gabriel's eyes widened. "What is this? Is this your man? I didn't know—"

I shook my head. "Oh gods no. You have a bounty on your head, and we are here to collect it. Now get off my partner"—I went through the different words in my head—"but like, not that kind of partner. My work partner. Yeah, you know what I mean."

Gabriel held up his hands and got off Zach. I tried to look away from the bulge in Gabriel's pants. This was getting to be so awkward. I nodded over to the desk chair. "Sit over there."

He quickly did as I said. I looked over at Zach. "You okay over there?"

Zach sighed as he sat up. "Yeah, I'm all right. This guy's handsy though."

"Good. Wouldn't want you to lose your virginity on a job."

"Hey, I was just about to kill him if you didn't come in here. I wouldn't have lost my virginity."

"Sure." I gestured to Gabriel with my revolver. "Now, how should we deal with him?"

Gabriel fumbled on the ground as his dark eyes were turning red. "Please don't kill me. I'm young and have a lot going for me."

"Well," I began, "that's the problem. All the old men hate that you're stepping on their toes. You should have known better."

"I'll pay you double whatever you're working for! Please!"

I shook my head as Zach stood next to me. "Not that easy. We aren't just working for money but information as well. Unless you know the location of a Cornelius Adams, you really can't persuade us."

There was a look of confusion in our mark's eyes. "Wait, but I do know where he is! Please, just spare me!"

I stared at him for a long moment, then turned to Zach, who was just as perplexed. I couldn't believe it would be that easy, not to mention the odds were slim.

There was one way to find out the truth. "What's he look like?"

He let out a sigh that sounded a bit lovestruck. "He's beautiful. Eyes are as golden as both of yours and hair as white as the Sirian sand. He's got sharp features, a cocky grin, and can pull out his gun faster than anyone alive, among other things."

Both Zach and I were gaping at him. That sure sounded like Cor. Was this guy in love with him? And knew where he was?

Zach brought his finger to his lip. "So earlier when you said you were with another guy…"

Gabriel nodded. "Yeah, with Cor."

Zach started making gagging sounds and was wiping his tongue with his hands. "Oh, disgusting. I made out with someone who made out with Cor. I'm going to be sick."

I gave him a look. He shook his head. "No, you can't give me that look. I know the things you did together, so shut up."

Gabriel stared at the two of us. "Oh, were you two…?"

"It was a long time ago," I answered and bent down so our eyes were at the same level. "Now, how do I know you're telling the truth and that you will take me to him?"

He gulped and glanced over at Zach, who was still acting like he was going to vomit. "I… uh… He's on Zynon making sure there aren't… any… bounty hunters after me."

it would clear his name but never explained further. I thought maybe he got in a little trouble earlier but not something as big as this."

Zach laughed. "And you think we believe you?"

"What choice do you have?" Gabriel asked. "You either are going to believe me or kill me to get the information you want. I am just telling you what I know."

He had a point there.

I folded my arms in front of me. "Well then, how will we get proof you do, in fact, know Cor?"

Suddenly the telephone in the room rang. We all stared at it, not sure what to do.

CHAPTER XIV

Zach

We all stared at the phone. Who in the world would be calling at this hour?

"That's probably him," Gabriel commented. "He likes checking in to make sure I'm not murdered by some bounty hunters." He glared at us for a long moment.

Ellie's voice went a little cold. "Well, good to see he has the ability to care about someone other than himself."

I interjected before hatred swallowed Ellie whole. "If we answer, it will prove that he is with this guy here and that he can take us to him. What do you say, Ellie?"

She bit her lip. "You have a point. And it would be easier if we used this guy to get to him. I'm not sure if our contact would actually lead us in the right direction now that we have found out the truth…"

"But he'll be mad if Gabriel here shows up to Zynon…," I added, still not certain what we should do.

The phone rang again. Ellie gestured to it. "Answer, but don't let him know we are here. If you do a good job, we will spare your life. Also, put it on speaker."

Gabriel nodded and grabbed the phone. He turned it on speaker. "Hello?"

"Hey, sorry to call, I just wanted to check in."

Ellie visibly tensed, and I could feel my own body seize up. That was his voice—that was Cor's voice. We had finally found him.

Gabriel gulped. "No problem. I'm glad to hear from you. Was there any trouble on your end?"

"Just a little, but nothing I couldn't handle. How about you? Are you safe? I'm not interrupting anything, am I?"

"No, no. I'm chilling in my room. Saw a cute boy but

he wasn't interested. How about you? Did you find any clients for the night?"

Clients? Ellie and I glanced at each other, and I could see the grin forming on her lips. It all made sense now —why Gabriel thought she was a prostitute. Cor had been whoring out for money. Between that and the gambling, that was how Gabriel was getting enough money to become one of the elite.

This situation kept getting better and better.

"No," Cor answered. "I think I'm just going to check around and see if there are any other people hired to assassinate you. Promise me you will stay safe until you come up tomorrow. Don't do anything to gather attention."

"Oh, you know me. I tend to stay out of the limelight."

"Yeah, right. Anyway, have a good night, and I love you."

"Love you too." Gabriel hung up the phone.

I glanced over to Ellie to find her clenching her jaw. I didn't know what it was like to hear the man you once loved—the man who betrayed her and destroyed our home—tell someone else they loved them. I didn't particularly want to.

CHAPTER XV

Cor

I hung up the phone, feeling a little better after hearing Gabe's voice. Something felt off, however, and I couldn't quite get all the worry out of my system. He wouldn't have answered the phone, though, if there was someone in the room. But then again, why did he put me on speaker?

I prayed to the gods he was all right.

Knowing I couldn't do anything more from up here, I decided I needed to get rid of the bodies quickly. The best way to do that was to dump them outside the giant dome over the casino as then the lack of atmosphere and low gravity would carry their bodies off to be completely destroyed. The problem was getting them to a chute to do just that. I glanced over at the bodies and sighed. They were such big men too.

I transformed into a Silurian as I knew I wouldn't get questioned about carrying around a huge bag disguised as one of them. It wasn't because they were trustworthy or anything but more that no one wanted to get on their bad side.

Searching through the cabinets, I found some large trash bags, which I didn't question as the hotel was used to host large parties and provided them to guests to throw away everything. On the side of the box, I noticed it said compostable, which was good because the rest of what I was throwing away was compostable as well.

I double-checked the pockets of the two men but found nothing else. They must have had a room they were staying in or something. The information would be on the ID cards that I'd taken. I would just need to bring the cards down later and sneak onto one of the computers at the front desk. Hopefully then I would find who sent them, although I knew there were multiple humans who wanted my sweet Gabe dead. I sighed as I crammed the first body into the bag. He barely fit, but the bag didn't rip. These were definitely some hefty compostable bags.

As I dragged the body into the hallway, I remembered that all the floors had a trash chute. I thanked the gods as I did not want to lug this all the way downstairs and hope that no one noticed my eyes. I pulled the bag down the hallway, and although I was transformed into a Silurian, I didn't have the same strength, and this man was rather large. Luckily, since it was just before dinner, no one was around to question me or tell the staff what I was doing. I made it down the corridor with no problems and stuffed him into the chute. After a push of a button, the body was gone.

Now I just needed to dump the other body.

The other body was heavier, but I was able to get it into the chute just fine. No one spotted me as they were upstairs at the restaurant that overlooked the moon in all its glory or gambling. At the thought of dinner, my stomach grumbled. It was time for something to eat, especially after the workout I just had.

I went back into my room and shifted into my normal

Kausian form. As I stepped inside, I realized there was still the matter of the blood to deal with. Thank goodness the tile was black. I moved over to the faucet and grabbed some towels and soap to clean the area. I would have to throw the towels down the chute as well so I wouldn't have to worry about anyone finding them, not that it really mattered since everyone wanted us dead anyway.

It didn't take long to wipe up the mess as I was used to cleaning up bodies, unfortunately. Once I was done, I changed into my more formal wear, hooked on my revolver, pocketed the two IDs I had just in case someone came back looking for them, and headed up to the roof.

As the doors of the elevator opened, I gaped at the view that this glass-enclosed establishment provided. I always forgot how amazing it was to see the planet Maldek from the moon. It seemed so distant even though I had been there hours before. It was a miracle that any of the races could make it all the way up here when there were parts of our world that weren't even habitable—three-quarters of it. I guess when those with money wanted to go to space, they did just that.

Not like I was complaining—this place was a lot

more magnificent than the one-hundred-below-freezing poles, the continent of pure lava, or the areas that had a hurricane every few days. The moon, because of the way the world and moon were created, always faced the planet, and the planet always spun at the same speed. This caused the moon to always show the same side, and Maldek always appeared the same from up here. Physics was crazy like that.

I could make out all the different zones and even see the walls that the zones had constructed and the force fields, depending on the area. Well, I could see all the zones except the Sirian Zone since it was underwater. All the other areas were rather green.

Other than that large beige area.

I knew what that territory was, and it made my chest ache every time I saw it. The remnants of Kaus. I tried to bury those memories into the back of my mind when I saw a familiar face—the Silurian Krax.

His serpent lips turned up into a sly grin as he waved me over to join him. He and a human and Lyran were all sitting at a table with a glass of herbal wine. As I stepped up to their table, the faint smell of clove and cinnamon hit my nose. It was some potent stuff to have before dinner.

"Come sit with us and have a drink." Krax gestured to the empty chair.

I nodded, knowing I couldn't decline. "Of course."

He handed me a glass, and I took a sip, the spicy, earthy tones instantly making my tongue feel numb. I preferred berry wine myself but never declined an offer, especially one by Krax.

Krax was an elderly Silurian—one I didn't care to cross paths with but regularly did, and he always had a job for me that I couldn't refuse. Typically elderly Silurian were killed by ones in their prime, but Krax was still stronger than them, even at his age. His scales were lighter colored, and his eyes were glossier than a typical Silurian. Although I wanted to see him dead, I was glad he was alive so I'd get to enact my revenge on him.

"Now, how is my favorite Kausian?" His tongue slithered in his mouth. I gulped as I glanced over to the other two. They didn't seem to care that I was from Kaus as they paid it no mind. I still had my sunglasses on, but Krax already knew me.

"I'm fine. Thank you for asking. And how are you?"

"I'm good. Very good. We will be initiating new members this week, you know. My son will soon be joining this group along with your friend Gabriel."

That was when the human of the group reacted. I saw his eyes flicker with a little hatred, but he hid it shortly after. That didn't mean he had anything to do with the men in the room as many of the humans hated Gabriel. I still wasn't completely sure why, but I had my suspicions. Neither of us really liked to talk about our pasts, and so I never brought it up.

"I'm glad to hear your son is growing up to be just like you."

The Silurian laughed and slammed my back with his large reptilian hand. "I like you, Cornelius. You are one of the few Kausians I can enjoy, and you know why that is?"

I held back any sly comments. "I do not."

"Sure you do! It's because you will do anything to save your own skin. I guess, if truth be told, you're the only Kausian worth talking to. You are willing to sell out your entire nation for your own life."

I frowned, not wanting the memories to resurface. "I was just a kid. I didn't understand what was going to happen."

"Yet you still helped me and my men. I'm indebted to you, which is the only reason your friend Gabriel is on this moon. Where is he? Where is your pet human?"

I sipped my wine. It tasted worse with each passing moment. "He's still on the planet. I thought I would come up here and make sure the area was clear for him."

He laughed. "I see. And was it clear?"

"It is now."

The human shifted in his seat. So it was him. Now I knew who to monitor—and who to threaten. At least I wouldn't have to sneak into the front desk later. The Lyran paid the conversation no mind and drank the rest of his wine. Although Lyrans could be feisty, I found them to be the easiest to be around as long as you knew what not to do.

"Well, I'm glad we have someone like you around. It keeps everything a lot more entertaining. But I do have something to discuss with you, Cornelius. If you have the time later, please stop by my room. Let's say midnight?"

"A job offer, I presume?"

He swirled his wine. "Of sorts. I'll go over the details when we meet."

I held up my glass to him. "Well, I look forward to it. In the meantime, I'll let you get back to your dinner..."

"Nonsense, you may stay with us. I'm sure my two colleagues won't mind."

The human made a face like he would put up with my existence but did not enjoy it, whereas the Lyran raised his glass, his arm a little wobbly. It seemed he had too much to drink already. No wonder he hadn't made a fuss.

I leaned back in my chair. "Well, then I guess I'll stay for dinner."

CHAPTER XVI

Gabe

So that happened.

Cor was going to be so mad when I got up to Zynon. He didn't like surprises, especially ones involving me almost being killed. And it wouldn't be the first time either. Last time he was able to kill the bounty hunter before he murdered both of us, but that was different—that bounty hunter wasn't a Kausian.

And apparently they knew each other. Cor never talked about his past, which I didn't either, so it didn't bother me. However, they said he led to the destruction of Kaus, and I couldn't believe that. No, he was innocent, or at most there was more to the story. Once we got up to Zynon, he would tell us what happened and it would be cleared up.

At least that was what I hoped.

What really bothered me was the fact that it was *that man* who hired these two bounty hunters—Byron Hill. I wrinkled my nose at the thought of him. I hated him with a passion. He had made my life miserable—he had made me want to kill myself because of what I was. He made me feel as if I didn't deserve a life on this planet. It was why I ran away when I was fifteen—to get away from him.

But my mother always found me. And then so would he.

I should probably tell the truth about Byron, but I didn't want that sort of pity. No, I would hold off until it was safe—until I knew he would understand. He had his own secrets—he would accept mine.

But right now I had to deal with the fact that one of the people who had tried to kill me was dragging me to the post office. It was dark, and there weren't too many people wandering around, just some couples here and there and a few loners who kept their eyes out for anyone who might seem dangerous. I took a breath of the crisp night air. I loved summer nights; they made one feel alive.

Zach, one of my captors, walked with me, whistling as he clapped and snapped his hands together. He seemed awkward and nervous. It made me smile a little.

"You know," I began. "We could ditch this and go back to the hotel room."

He quickly shook his head. "Nope, not doing that again."

"Oh, but you are so cute."

His cheeks turned a beet red. "No, that's not my thing."

"But you and that girl aren't together—"

"No, I don't want a relationship. Or at least not a sexual one. Ellie and I have a close friendship, and I can't imagine anything more with anyone. She is my other half, in a way, but like in a siblings sort of way if I had to describe it. It's different from that, though, as I like being close to her and hearing her problems. We cuddle and sleep in the same bed, but it's never sexual. The two of us have always known each other and have been through a lot."

I smiled. "That sounds like the purest love of all."

"We never fight—that is, unless there is only one slice of pie left. Then all bets are off."

Laughing, I wondered if I would ever find someone to be that close to. Cor and I were close, but not like that. Before him, I had no friends or loves—I even felt distant to my mother. And my father…

"I'm sorry your kind has been treated like dirt. It's unfair."

"Well, thanks for not treating us like dirt. But as far as everyone else is concerned, you don't have to say sorry. It isn't your fault the world is full of assholes."

"Ain't that the truth."

We kept moving forward, and I could see the post office in the distance. Post offices on the edge of zones were normally open until late since there were a lot of trading and shipping needs, not to mention wiring money to someone like we were doing.

To Byron himself.

I wanted to tell them it wouldn't matter and that Byron would kill them either way and would try to kill me again. I needed to distract myself.

"You don't seem like killers. How long have you been bounty hunters?" I asked.

Zach shrugged. "We do what we can to survive. We have been at it for three years for money. You know, instead of prostitution."

"Of course. Two most-needed jobs—bounty hunting and prostitution."

"Exactly. And no one cares who you hire for either as long as you get the job done."

I laughed. "I like you, Zach. You are funny."

"Thank you. I try."

We made it to the post office, and Zach filled out the paperwork while I pulled out my ID card. I scanned it on the tablet and accessed my accounts. It wasn't as if I could bring as much gold as they needed to wire over. No one carried around that much cash.

"Damn, how much money do you have?" Zach peered over my shoulder.

I jumped a little, not expecting him to fill out the form so quickly. I coughed. "These are my emergency funds. I rarely use them unless I am in a situation where I have to give a sum of money."

That was partially the truth. To be honest, it was my mother's account, and I had access to it if I needed. She had never seemed to notice if I spent some here or there, and it wasn't like she was going to run out.

Besides, she said she would help me any way she could.

"Emergency funds, eh? That seems nice."

"Yeah. It is. But again, I don't like using them."

He nodded as he handed me the paper he filled out. "I'm not sure what else to do with this. I haven't had to send such a large wire transfer before."

I checked over the slip, and he had filled out as much as he could. "You did everything right."

Zach grinned widely. "Sweet. Then we can rid ourselves of him."

Yeah, that wasn't going to work. You couldn't go back on your word when it came to Byron—especially since he wanted me dead. But I didn't want to tell them that—I didn't want to tell them what dangers they faced as they might go ahead and assassinate me.

"As for what to pay you for keeping me alive," I began, "what is your cost?"

Zach shrugged. "For now, just providing everything we need as we go to Zynon. Depending on how hectic it is, we can discuss payment after. We have to keep alive first, don't we?"

He had a point there. "Great. Yeah, I can pay for your way and cover the cost of everything, no problem. We will just need to get IDs next. I know a guy near here."

"Sounds good. This should work out then. Besides, why we really took the job from Byron was so we could find Cor, but you are helping us with that instead. This way we don't have more blood on our hands."

Right. Cor. I still wasn't sure what they wanted with him. I just prayed they would let him explain before doing anything rash. Although they got the better of me, I highly doubted they could take down Cor. I had nothing to worry about.

At least, that's what I hoped.

CHAPTER XVII

Ellie

Why did things always get so complicated?

Every mission we had been on, something happened, whether it be a setup, the person didn't actually have money to pay us, the target jumped off a bridge, it was another setup… Yeah, that last one happened a lot since we had a bounty on our heads in some places. Well, most places. But the fact that we had made it on our own for the past three years impressed our contractors and harbored a sense of trust that we would get the job done.

But now that wasn't exactly going to happen.

We had never backed out of a job like this. Well, that wasn't completely true, but that was a different circumstance and had to do with the fact we don't hurt animals. That Sirian was really afraid of cats.

Instead of calling Byron, we decided to just send the money we owed him through a wire transfer, including the cost of the bullets. It wasn't like he wouldn't figure it out once he was up on Zynon. And he would see our faces and send some other bounty hunter after us. Yeah, this wouldn't end well. But that was life for us.

While Zach dealt with sending the money back and watching Gabriel, who was also helping cover the cost because we had already spent some of the cash, I went over to pay the lodging for our horses for a couple of weeks since we wouldn't need them where we were heading tomorrow. The owner seemed to be confused, as we had told him we needed to leave as soon as possible because Zach's fake wife was pregnant. He didn't object, however, as I paid him well worth his time and then some. Not on our dime, of course, as Gabriel was quite wealthy.

Gabriel would also get us some tickets to go up to

Zynon tomorrow with him. I was not looking forward
to that, as I hated riding in that flying machine thing. It
just made me so utterly sick. I remembered Zach, Cor,
and I had to share a bucket to vomit in while we rode
up to the amusement park. Other than the traveling, it
had been a fun trip, even after we got arrested.

I tried not to smile at the memory, as I didn't like to
think fondly of Cor, but he was honestly in all my
enjoyable memories. He had meant the world to me,
and then he just disappeared. Deep in my heart, I
wanted to believe he was innocent, but as the weeks
and months went by, the more that sliver of my heart
died. Gabe had said he was working all the time to clear
his name, except I had a hard time believing that.

I grasped the ring at the end of my necklace. Cor had
a boyfriend. It had been three years, but it still stung
deep down a little. He had once said I meant the world
to him, but was that all a lie? Could someone move on
and no longer love as strongly as they did? I supposed
that was the case for me, as my feelings had changed
over the years. Zach was right—I needed to let go. But
it was too hard. I desired to know the truth.

I headed back toward the parlor and hotel as it was
where I would be meeting Zach and Gabe, when I

noticed a couple of men tailing me. They weren't stealthy, per the Silurian way. What they lacked in stealth, they made up with brute force, however.

But even if I knew they were there, this was not a good sign.

When we tried to leave the Lyran Zone, the guards had mentioned we were wanted for murdering those Silurians at the bar. The only problem was, we didn't do it. When we left there, everyone was still alive—just tranked. So there were two options—those Silurians were mad we got the better of them and claimed we killed someone, or someone came and killed them and made it look like it was us to set us up.

The question was, who could have done such a thing?

I pondered those thoughts as I debated what to do for a room. We couldn't exactly leave Gabriel alone for the night as he might run away. But at the same time, I didn't want to stay up and watch him all night. And now we had some Silurians trying to more than likely kill us.

Biting my lip, I wondered if it was a bad idea to lodge the horses. We should have grabbed them and run out of town. Then again, I doubted Gabriel would last out there. And I couldn't kill the Silurians as then more would come for us.

Perhaps there were overnight tickets to Zynon. I cringed at the thought of traveling. I hated traveling. It always made me sick, and I'd rather go during the day as I knew I wouldn't be able to sleep. But if these guys were just going to murder us in our sleep anyway, then it wasn't as if I were going to get any rest. Besides, there was plenty to do on the night ships between the casinos and bars. And there were shops where I could get some clothes to fit in on Zynon. I wasn't looking forward to having to wear dresses as most of the women in high society did.

Turning to meet up with Zach, I noticed the two Silurians were still tailing me. Should I lead them all the way back to Zach, or should I take care of them here and now? I could just transform, and no one would be the wiser. It wasn't like they were going to stop following me and try to take Zach out as well. Hopefully, these were the only two.

I made my way down a dark alley, and they followed. Idiots. I transformed into a Silurian and faced them with a bit of a smile.

They jumped a little, as if they hadn't encountered a Kausian before. Most people bolted when they first saw one of us transform, or told the cops since it was illegal. I didn't care right now since no one could see from the street, and I had a feeling I would have to kill these guys either way.

Both of them pulled out their guns and pointed them at me. "We are getting revenge for our friends you killed in the Lyran Zone."

I shook my head. "I didn't kill your friends. This is all a misunderstanding."

"But you did! We saw the bodies!"

So someone did murder them after we left. Now that was another mystery I would have to solve. But later. "Well, in for a penny."

Without hesitation, I shot them both in the head. They went down with loud thuds. I knew this was going to cause even more problems for us in the long run, but it wasn't like they were going to let me leave unharmed. With a sigh, I lifted them up and threw them in the large trash container. It would be a few days before anyone found them, but if all the Silurians were on alert for us, that wouldn't be a good thing.

It goes without saying that the Silurian race hated us the most. They were the ones who destroyed our home, after all. They turned all the other races against us and got the go-ahead to blow the place to smithereens. But they had to have had help—someone must have given them the codes. And the only person who could have done that was Cor.

But we had almost found him. We discovered his boyfriend, and he was going to lead us to Cor. We had done it, and I would shoot him the moment I saw him, and that would be that.

Taking a deep breath and letting it out slowly, I transformed back into my normal appearance. Now I would have to tell Zach everything that had happened. I wasn't looking forward to that—not to mention we needed to get out of here pronto.

I made my way to the nearest post office, hoping that was the one where Zach went to send the money. As I entered, I found Zach was still talking to a clerk. Gabriel was with him, staying quiet and out of the way. Zach had on his glasses, which reminded me to put on my own before people noticed my eyes. It was pitch-dark out, so it wasn't like we wouldn't stand out already with them on, but it helped some. Instead of thinking we were Kausian, they would think we were up to no good. That was much better.

Zach finished up the note for Byron and turned to

find me standing there. I smiled innocently, and he simply rolled his eyes.

"What did you do?" he asked as we stepped outside. Both suns had set now, and the air was beginning to cool down, which felt nice on my sweating skin.

I placed my hands on my upper chest. "I did nothing. But some Silurians were tailing me, and I might have had to take them out. They claimed we killed those Silurians in the bar."

He shook his head. "We didn't. We wouldn't waste bullets in a fight like that."

"That's what I said. But I had to silence them since they didn't seem like they were going to stop. But I have a feeling more will be on their way."

Gabriel interrupted. "So what you're saying is there's Silurians out to get you."

Zach and I glanced at each other, debating on whether that was the right word. I answered, "More or less. We're kind of like outlaws because we are bounty hunters."

"Bounty hunters that were hired to kill me."

I nodded. "Yup. But all this is to find our dear friend Cor." I slapped his back. "So you're lucky you had something to offer us. Besides, you got us some IDs right? Nothing should go wrong."

Gabriel sort of smiled and then frowned at the realization of how close he was to death. "I don't know if that is reassuring or not."

This time, Zach slapped his back. "Look at it this way. You now have two of the best bounty hunters making sure no one kills you."

"Great. Anyway, we still need to go get IDs. We should be able to get on the transport and into the casino no problem. However, if the Silurians know what you look like, I am not sure how that is going to help."

He had a point there. I shrugged. "They haven't killed us yet. But I think we should keep moving. Do you have anything personal that you want from the hotel? I'm thinking we should grab a night ticket to Zynon."

Gabriel sighed. "Yeah, let me pack real quick. And call Cor so he knows I'm on my way up. He's going to be suspicious."

"Just tell him it's because you miss him so very much. I mean, flattery always seems to work on him." I smiled. Zach simply rolled his eyes.

Gabriel eyed me suspiciously for a moment. "How

do the two of you know Cor again?"

"Best of friends, the three of us. We always got in all sorts of mischief."

"Right… Then how come he's never mentioned you two?"

I had to admit, that stung a little. I shrugged. "Does he mention anything about Kaus? He probably thought we were dead and didn't want to bring back up horrible memories."

"You have a point. He has mentioned nothing about Kaus or anyone from there. I guess if he thought you were dead…"

Zach grinned. "And I can't wait to see his face. I bet he's going to be ecstatic to see that we aren't dead."

I knew Zach was being sarcastic, but Gabriel nodded in agreement. "Yeah, if you all were as close as you say, I bet he will. To be honest, he's been lonely all the time I've been with him. There's a void I can't fill. He tries to hide it, but I can see it, deep down. Once you hear his story, I know you all will find out what transpired."

I wanted to vomit from those words. It was his fault all this happened. I clutched my hand into a fist but grinned. "Yeah, I'm sure his story will straighten everything out."

CHAPTER XVIII

<u>**Zach**</u>

We found Cor's boyfriend. We heard Cor on the phone. There were Silurians after us, saying we murdered their kind. And more than likely, Byron was going to send men after us.

So this mission is going about normal.

I pinched the bridge of my nose as I followed Ellie and Gabriel toward the ticket booth with our fake IDs. There were quite a few people out, but then I realized it was because we were in the trading district and there was always something happening at night in the summer. I wondered what it would be like having a home and getting to enjoy these things on a regular basis. I bet it was fun.

Making our way through the town toward where the spaceport was, I prayed to the gods that there was a flight leaving soon. I didn't want to wait around and see if there were more Silurians after us, not to mention the possibility of Byron sending more than one bounty hunter after Gabriel. We needed out of here—fast.

None of us was sure what time a ship would leave during the night as it took six hours to travel up to the moon and then another six hours to come back. I glanced up at the moon, wanting more than anything not to go on that retched machine. I hated flying, even though I had only done it twice before when Ellie and Cor took me to the amusement park. And by take me, I mean we all sneaked in, which was probably one of our biggest feats yet. The first time, at least. The second time was a different story—that was why we were on their Do Not Let In posters.

We arrived at the ticket office. We checked the screens and found that there was, in fact, a transport leaving within the hour. Gabriel paid for the tickets, and we boarded with the rest of the tired and wicked. The tired ones were mainly families that wanted a cheaper ticket so they could enjoy the amusement park even more. The wicked, on the other hand, were the ones traveling to the casino and hotel. Only the elite could take part in the casino, which meant that Gabriel would have to act like we were his bodyguards or something, which we were, so that wasn't much of a problem. We would just have to play the so-called society gentleman and lady part, which also meant Ellie would have to find herself a nice dress, and I would have to find some clothes that were better suited. I didn't mind, but Ellie was so going to throw a fit.

Of which she threw a fit when we had to turn in our guns.

We had to do it nevertheless as there were no weapons allowed on the ship. I had a feeling there were knives all around us, though, including the one tucked in Ellie's book. But a gun was different—a gun could pierce the hull and we could all die. It made sense why we had to check them in as we boarded.

"I better get my gun back, Zach. Crazy Jack has saved my life many times."

I patted her back as we stepped into the ship. "I

know, Ellie, I know. Just like my Lucky Susan."

There were two parts of the transport, and depending on what type of ticket we had, we would either be stuck with all the families or with the high class who wanted us dead. I wasn't sure which Gabriel bought tickets for, but as we followed him through the transport, we found he opted for the business. I didn't know if that was because he felt safer around people like himself or because he just wanted a nice bed.

The ship was large—at least as big as a market plus the surrounding buildings that would be hotels or where the workers worked on whatever was needed for a ship like this to run. There were hundreds of people of all the different races. Except Kausian, of course. The smell of barbecue filled my nostrils, and I made a note of where the booth was so I could circle back around later. I hadn't had good barbecue in forever. It took all my willpower not to drool.

It was apparent what part of the ship was for the public and which was for those with money. Gabriel showed his identification to what appeared to be a security guard, and the door opened to a whole different world. Smoke from all types of cigars and cigarettes filled the air, and I held back a cough. There was laughter and the sound of chips and dice rolling.

There were shops like in the other areas, but these were a lot higher class. There were a few clothing shops, so both Ellie and I were in luck as we were already getting stares, and not just because of the sunglasses we were wearing in the middle of the night.

Gabriel zigzagged through the tables and various rooms, and the two of us followed. We tried not to glance at all the different rich folk who made up the area. We didn't want to gather attention—mainly because we didn't know who wanted our heads at the moment. And we didn't need to add to the list.

We made it to some hallways, and Gabriel took out a key card that the ticket person must have given him, and the door slid open to reveal a modest room with a full-sized bed and a couch. There was a cramped bathroom/shower on the right and even a mini fridge. Ellie and I glanced at each other.

"So who gets the bed?" she asked.

Gabriel collapsed on the bed, and it was almost bouncy, like it was a fresh mattress. I didn't know when the last time I slept on a new mattress was. "Me, of course. You two can fight over the couch. That is unless Zach wants to share a bed with me."

I quickly shook my head. "Nope."

He laughed. "I was joking. For that part anyway. I'm in fact taking the bed."

I sighed. The bed looked soft. At least once we got to Zynon, we would get a nice bed. Hopefully. "I guess it doesn't matter since one of us will take watch."

Ellie slapped my shoulder. "That's the spirit. Now, are you going to go buy clothes first or shall I?"

"I guess I can." I held out my hand to Gabriel. "Money please!"

He rolled his eyes but handed me a card anyway. "Just make sure to get something flattering. I can come with you, if you want. I don't trust your sense of style. Actually, let's all go. I saw what you wore tonight, and it stood out like a sore thumb."

Ellie crossed her arms. "That was from a very expensive shop I'll have you know."

Gabriel sighed. "Yeah, yeah. That's what they all say. Just let me pick it out."

"Says the guy with a flashy green hat?" Ellie countered.

"The hat looks good, and my suit is perfect. And I dress Cor up for his job."

I pressed my fist on my palm as if I had a thought.

"Oh, that reminds me. Can you give me a specific word for what he does?"

"He's a prostitute."

I bent over, laughing. I still couldn't believe it. Cor was a prostitute. I didn't have anything against the job, but to hear someone whom you were searching for after so long and someone you had grown up with was one was hysterical. This whole time in our minds he was out there killing people and causing chaos when really he was just hooking up with random men and women.

"What's so funny? Many people like sleeping with Kausians since they can change into whatever they want," Gabriel explained.

There was so much wrong with that comment, but I wasn't even going to start. "Okay, I'm done laughing. Let's go."

CHAPTER XIX

Gabe

We headed back toward where the shops were. In this section of the ship everything was high end which was exactly what we needed to make these two not stand out more than they already did. Getting Ellie in a dress would be the first step, but the two of them carried themselves in a way that didn't quite fit with the rest of this cabin. I wasn't sure if it was because Kausians always seemed to get dizzy and sick on ships or if that was just their normal stride.

Either way, we would have to work on it.

It didn't take too long for Cor to learn all the tricks, but he'd mentioned he had some training already. By the looks of it, these two did not have the same schooling. People stared as I led them through the corridors and lounge. Soon they wouldn't even recognize them, so I didn't have to worry about it too much.

We made it to one of the clothing shops, and I went through the dresses. These were all mass produced, but that would be fine. We didn't have time for a tailor. I picked out a few different colors—all bold and on the darker side as she didn't strike me as someone who would wear pastels. After gathering a few, I handed them to Ellie.

"Try these on and make sure they fit. As for what to wear the rest of the time on the ship…" I bit my lip. We didn't need anything too fancy yet, so I pulled out the most simple one and placed it on top. It was a blue top with some lace with a dark blue-and-black shirt. "Wear this one."

Ellie rolled her eyes. "Just because I am a woman doesn't mean I should have to wear a dress or skirt. Why can't I wear a suit?"

"Have you seen any women around here wearing suits?"

"Well, no…"

"Exactly. We are in a shark tank currently, and if you don't want to be spotted by anyone, including the Silurians who are after you, then you will wear a skirt."

She made a loud, audible sigh, and went to the dressing room with no more complaints. At least she listened to reason.

Zach whistled. "I have to hand it to you—you know how to handle her."

"She's a smart woman, and smart women listen to reason. It's as simple as that."

"Fair enough. She is definitely the smartest woman I have ever known."

He said that with a bit of a proud voice. It made me smile a little.

"As for you…" I pulled a gray frock coat off a hanger, black dress pants, a blue vest similar to Ellie's skirt, a white shirt, and a white satin puff tie and handed it all to Zach. "Go try those on."

He stared for a moment as if he had never seen such fine clothes. He wiped his hands off on his pants and then grabbed them.

"I will be right back then."

With that, he went into a changing room. I snatched a few more outfits for him. I didn't need him to try them all on since I knew his size—I had been staring at his figure for a couple of hours now, after all.

I leaned against the wall as I waited for the two of them to be finished. After a while, Ellie stuck her head out of the door.

"I need a little help putting all this on...," she admitted.

One of the shop attendants went to her and helped her try the clothes on. I should have figured—she wasn't used to the circus act that was putting on women's dresses. I did not envy her.

A few minutes later, both of them stepped out of the changing rooms in their new outfits. Zach was tugging on his vest as if it were uncomfortable, but from what I could tell, it fit perfectly. Ellie had her hands on her hips as she gave me an annoyed look.

"There is no way I'm going to stay in this. I don't even have free range of my legs!"

I let out a sigh. "But think of how many weapons you can hide under your petticoat."

Her eyes widened as she patted her legs. "Wow.

You're right."

Zach laughed as he shook his head. "You appear lovely, Ellie. Just admit you like the dress."

She took the moment to check out Zach's outfit, then whistled. "Looking fine there, Zach. You could get all the ladies and gentlemen kissing your feet."

He ran his fingers through his ginger hair, which was still a mess. I would have to fix that later. "Well, I don't blame them. I am pretty handsome."

I gave him a wink. "I won't deny that."

The comment made him turn beat red, and I turned to pay for all the clothes we bought. I also added a suitcase since we would need to lug these to the hotel on Zynon somehow. The cashier, an elderly Lyran, tallied everything up, and I paid with a tap of my card. As she folded and put the clothes away, I handed Ellie a hat and some lace gloves I had picked up.

"I think these will add to the look. What do you think?"

She shrugged. "Don't know. Never was one for fashion."

"And for your eyes…" I handed Ellie the pair of delicate glasses that were a light shade of blue with a gold-colored frame. For Zach, I gave him a pair of red glasses that were rectangle-shaped and had a black frame.

"Ooh," Zach said as he took them and put them on. He grinned widely at Ellie. "Pretty cunning, don't ya think?"

She shook her head. "You just think you're the shit, don't you?"

He straightened his collar. "Damn straight. You wish you were as handsome as me."

"No, I wish I was wearing pants." She turned to me. "Are you sure I can't wear pants?"

I nodded. "No woman in proper society wears pants. You would stand out."

Zach grabbed the luggage, and we made our way through the ship back to where our room was. As we passed the gambling lounge, Ellie stopped.

"Hey, maybe we should—" Before she finished her sentence, the ship moved. She put her hand over her mouth and ran toward the room. I hurried after her since I was the one who had the key.

As I caught up to her, she was moving back and forth in place, as if that would stop her from actually throwing up. I quickly unlocked the door, and she tore into the bathroom and closed the door. Poor Kausians and their motion sickness.

I was about to turn and ask Zach if he was all right when I saw his pale face. I sighed as I nodded to the bucket.

"Go ahead and throw up in that."

He set down the luggage and grabbed the bucket to go join Ellie in the bathroom. I let out a sigh as I locked our door and collapsed on the bed. After having spent a few hours with them both, I couldn't believe they had first been sent to kill me. They were kind, funny, and had a dynamic that I was most jealous of. Was that what best friends were like—is that what it was like to have a family?

I rolled over and picked up the phone. The two of them would need something with ginger in it, not to mention something to eat as it sounded like their stomachs were now empty. Only a few more hours until we arrived—might as well make the best of it.

CHAPTER XX

<u>Cor</u>

I had some sort of vegetable risotto with an herb-rubbed chicken breast for dinner. It was wonderful, as food in this place was always tasty, but I couldn't enjoy it with Krax sitting across from me, not to mention the human who had almost caused my death. I was used to the latter, though, but with Krax, it was personal.

He was the person I wanted to make suffer.

And to do that, I had to kiss his scaly ass until the time was right. I felt that day was coming soon, however, and I would relish in his agony. But I had to remind myself to work one step at a time and not to let on anything was going on.

After dinner, I headed down to the poker tables to make a bit of cash and to practice for the tournament that was to start in a couple of days. That was one reason we were up here a week before the initiation ceremony—because they had a big tournament that anyone could join. It was high stakes, but I loved a good challenge. Besides, between my winning streaks and nightly activities, I had more than enough to buy in for Gabe and me.

I had won a few rounds and made a bit of money before I noticed the clock was nearing midnight. Krax had invited—more like ordered—me to come to his room for after-dinner drinks. I didn't particularly want to attend but knew it was much more than that. He was going to give me a job—a job I couldn't say no to. But at least it would pay well, which was one way Gabe and I could pull all this off.

Gabe didn't know that, however. He thought most of the money I provided was through entertaining women and men. While that helped pay bills, there was no way it would cover everything we needed to pull off him being part of this elite club. And once he would be indoctrinated, I could move to the next part of my plan.

Keeping an eye out and making sure no one followed me and that there weren't any more assassins after me, I weaved through the hotel part of the casino up to Krax's room. It wasn't the first time I had been there, and it wouldn't be the last. All for business, of course. He wouldn't want to associate with a Kausian, or any non-Silurian, otherwise.

The hotel was broken up into parts—a human floor, a Sirian floor, a Lyran floor, and a Silurian floor. I didn't agree with such segregation, but it seemed to keep the drunk fistfights down, at least on the hotel levels. The casino and dinning floors, however, were a completely different story.

Once I got off the Silurian level, I was immediately welcomed with guns and glares. There were half a dozen Silurians guarding the hallway, and they were quicker to shoot than use their brains. I raised my hands slowly as I heard Krax's voice come from down the corridor.

"He is welcome. Let him through."

I let out a breath as the guns lowered a tad, and I could walk through the hallway with less of a worry.

There were still some that had their gun pointed at me, but it was more of a warning than they were going to fire right then and there. It didn't make me feel better, however.

As I stepped into the room Krax had left open, I found three other Silurians in his suite as well, as if they had been discussing some important business. I gulped, not enjoying being around this many of their kind without some sort of backup or at least another gun.

"I'll make this quick since it's late and it's a rather straightforward job," Krax explained as he grabbed some folders. "I need you to assassinate these two Kausians. It seems they have attacked and killed some Silurians while they were in the Lyran Zone. You can manage that, right? They aren't the first Kausians we have had you go after."

I let out a slow breath, reminding myself it was all for the greater good. "No, they aren't."

"Excellent. You can deal with this after Gabriel is indoctrinated. And then you will have everything you wanted. Status, money, power. It will be all yours."

Nodding, I flipped through the folders. As I saw the photos of the two Kausians, I felt my heart drop into my stomach.

Elvira and Zachariah.

I shut the folders. "What did they do exactly?"

"They shot up a bar. Killed some very important men to me. Why, is there a problem?"

I wanted to say yes, but I knew that wouldn't end well for me. I would have to figure out some way to make this work and not kill them; otherwise, Krax would send someone else after them. "No. They just don't look like killers."

He wrapped his arm around my shoulder. "Well, as you know, looks can be deceiving. I mean, look at you. You seem kind and not someone who caused the destruction of his home, and yet, here you are. Three years after giving me the codes to enter your zone."

It felt like another punch to the gut. "That's not—"

"I'll give you a month to hunt them down. If I don't hear from you, I'll send someone else and you can kiss Gabriel goodbye. Do we have a deal? Oh, and of course your usual cost and whatnot."

I slowly nodded. "Yeah, we have a deal."

"That's good to hear. I wouldn't have it any other way." It was more of a threat than an agreement. I gulped and took the folders with me as I left his room before he could press any further. By the narrowing of his reptilian eyes, he knew something was up.

Heading to the human area of the hotel, I wasn't sure what I should worry about first. Gabe was probably fine —he more than likely had someone he hooked up with for the night to feel a little safer. Then he would head up here in the morning, and all would be well. I would just have to keep him safe for a little longer, and I could have my revenge on Krax. After that, I doubted he would want anything to do with a person like me.

I got to my room and checked to make sure no one was waiting to murder me again. I had grown good at finding all the potential spots someone could hide. Deciding it was clear for now, I tossed the folders on the bed and collapsed next to them.

I pulled my ring out of my pocket and stared at the worn wood I had carved what felt like another lifetime ago. There was no way I was going to assassinate Ellie and Zach. They were the two people I cared about most. Not that they would consider me as one of their friends ever again. I couldn't blame them. I had been stupid and trusted the wrong person. But I would make it right. I had to.

Which meant I had a month to get all the info I needed to eradicate the Silurian Zone. They were the ones who destroyed my home, and in turn I would wipe out theirs. It was only fair. The problem had always been no one was allowed in the Silurian Zone except Silurians. And they checked everyone's eyes to make sure no one was Kausian. I had already tried and barely escaped with my life. However, those who were part of the society could be invited in. All I required was for Krax to let me in, and then I could destroy the city with their own weapons of war.

Then they could all die in a fiery explosion, just like my people had.

I turned over and flipped through the folders. These two little shits had been on my tail this whole time. I had to hand it to Ellie—she was determined to find me. I couldn't blame her. It really looked like I had betrayed our kind. But it was so much more complicated than that. Either way, though, I had to make it right.

Gently sliding my finger over the photo of Ellie, I smiled a little. She had grown up but still had that glare that could murder a person. Her hair was long and a deep brown that I always loved. My heart ached a little as I had missed being around her and her quirkiness. I noted she was wearing men's clothing and chuckled. That was so like her.

I flipped through Zach's folder as well. His hair was a lot longer now and a bright ginger. I was glad to see he was much more confident about his hair as many Kausians shunned him for being half human. It shouldn't have mattered—they shouldn't have cared as all Kausians knew the feeling of being an outcast. That once-shy boy clearly was more outgoing. It was all thanks to Ellie, I suspected. She had changed both our lives.

Shutting the folders, I noticed the answering machine blinking. I leaned over and pressed the button.

"Hey, Cor. So I decided I'm going to come up early and am hopping on a ship within the hour. I should be up there in seven or so hours. You can check the transport board. See you soon!"

It was Gabe. I furrowed my eyebrows. That was strange. Why was he coming up earlier than planned? I had talked to him just a few hours before, and he mentioned nothing. Did he just miss me, or was there something more going on? I glanced at the clock. The message was left a good four hours ago, so I only had a couple of hours until he was here. I didn't feel like sleeping, which meant I could earn some money through blackjack or something more fun.

With a grin, I tucked the folders under the cushions of the couch and went back down to the casino, hoping to get lucky.

I straightened my vest as I closed the hotel door behind me. The Sirian woman, who I believed was named Jubilee, called out from her bed. "Good night, Cornelius."

I shut the door and headed toward where the transport docked for both the casino and the amusement park. It wasn't too far of a walk, and luckily not many were around as it was early morning now. It was going to be a long day after having spent all night eating, drinking, gambling, dealing with Krax, and sleeping with a beautiful young woman who, it just so happened, worked at the front desk. That might come in handy later. At least I could have the bartender make me an herbal tea to get me through the day. First thing was first, however. I needed to go retrieve Gabe before someone else did.

I made my way through the hallways of the casino. There weren't many people out as they would all be sleeping in front a night of, well, everything I had done and more. I yawned and stretched as I passed the front desk. Jubilee, of course, wasn't working yet, as she had the evening and night shift. I winked at the girl who was working the desk, though, and made the panther-like Lyran blush.

I stepped outside—or at least what I would consider outside as it was just a giant glass corridor that led to the spaceport. It always surprised me that the high class didn't have their own aisle but had to go down the same path. Granted, their exit off the ship made it so they didn't have to cut across the lower- and middle-class people as they rushed toward the park. I watched as children of all different races ran toward the theme park, their parents in tow, tired from the overnight transport. It made me smile a little as I remembered taking the night transport with Ellie and Zach when we snuck into the amusement park all those years ago. It wasn't an easy feat, but we managed with Ellie's devious mind.

Scanning the crowd, I looked for Gabe. He should be getting off the business class, especially if he took the night ride. Only the business class provided beds— comfy ones, might I add? More and more people got off the transport when finally I spotted him in a new green hat and waved him over.

I wasn't sure if it was the fact that I didn't expect them to be there or if my attention was solely on Gabe, but when a fist came flying toward my face, I realized Ellie was standing in front of me.

CHAPTER XXI

Ellie

All I could see was red. I tried to breathe, but it felt like no air was coming to me—as if I were outside on the moon itself. I was gasping as my ears rang. I didn't know if people around us were yelling or had even noticed me, but I could make out one sound—the voice of the man I had just punched as he rubbed the side of his face. He was on the ground since I had used all my strength on him and he clearly didn't see it coming.

"Ellie. What in the gods' names are you doing here?"

It was his voice—the voice of the boy who betrayed me—the voice of the bastard who betrayed our kind.

I didn't know what I wanted to do. I had been waiting so long for this moment. I knew I couldn't kill him right then and there as I would be arrested on the spot. But perhaps that would be worth it. Gabe had said he was trying to clear his name for something, and I wanted to hear him out, but years of pent-up rage were boiling out from my heart. Would his blood on my hands make it all go away? I wanted to curl into a ball and sob and beg him to explain what had happened—why he did it. I wanted to punch him and watch him bleed on the smooth metallic floor. I wanted to cause a scene. I wanted everyone to hear my anguish.

But most importantly, as of that moment, I wanted to breathe.

I collapsed on the ground, wheezing. Shit, why did I have to be so weak? This had never happened before—I never had any problems facing horrible men to claim the wanted-poster rewards. I never choked—I was strong and determined. Why now? Why in front of him of all people?

Cor reached out to help me. I slapped his hand before he could get near me.

"Don't touch me!"

Zach knelt down beside me. "Ellie, breathe, okay?"

I nodded, wanting to point out that I was clearly trying to, but it wasn't working. I presumed people were staring—why wouldn't they? Some fragile girl was having a panic attack. Typical in their eyes. Little did they know I could kill them all with my pinky if I had to.

Squeezing my eyes shut, I willed my lungs to work. I slowed my breathing, counting to ten in and counting to ten out. I had to calm down. I couldn't be this much of a weakling in front of Cor. I had to show him how determined I was—I had to show him how much I hated him. I took a few more breaths.

I could feel the tension subside. My vision cleared, and there were indeed people wondering what was happening, but it was fewer than I had worried about. Most of them were trying to get to their hotel rooms to rest a bit before continuing to the park, so they didn't stop to stare. At least I had that going for me. I blinked a few times to find Cor hadn't moved and was still sitting on the ground, waiting for me to calm down. I was surprised he didn't run off when he could. I knew I would. It made little sense.

His golden eyes stared at me, full of fear but also concern. It had been three years since I had seen him, and he was no longer that carefree teen I once knew but was a little more mature, and I could see the stress that he wore under his eyes. It would be a lie to say that he wasn't still attractive—in fact he was even more handsome than when we were together.

My heart felt as if it were literally ripping apart. What was wrong with me? Why was this so hard? Why did this hurt so much? I glanced down to find my hands trembling. Zach's hand rubbed my back. I was glad he was there—I wasn't sure what I would have done if he weren't by my side.

Cor's voice interrupted my thoughts. "We should get out of here. People are staring. Come with me, and we can discuss this in my room."

He wanted us to go with him? That made little sense. He had to realize why we were there—he had to know I wanted him to pay for what he had done. Did he really think himself innocent? Did he think I was going to be won over by some smiles and lies?

Or was he going to tell us everything?

"Okay," I said as Zach helped me up. "Let's talk."

"But first"—Cor held up his hand as if he was going

to say something but then decided not to. He turned his attention to Gabriel—"Gabe. I need a word with you real quick."

"Right, yeah. I guess I need to explain." Gabriel nodded, still perplexed I had punched Cor and then curled up into a hyperventilating ball. Gabriel went with him, however, and I watched as they discussed what happened. My guess was Cor wanted to know why Gabriel hadn't said anything about us. I saw as Gabriel explained, trying to be nonchalant about it, which seemed to be his thing. I still hadn't figured him out. He was afraid to die when it came to it, but his actions said otherwise. As he talked, Cor rubbed his face as if he couldn't deal with the stress that was Zach and me.

"So now what?" Zach whispered in my ear.

"We listen to his lies. See if we can figure out what really happened?"

"You think he will lie to us after all this time?"

"He's been running. I mean, look at him—he's weaved so many lies and plans he probably doesn't know which way is up anymore. I must admit I am curious though. If I were him, I would have run off the moment I saw us."

Zach chuckled. "Most would run away from you in general. But yes, I found that odd too. I don't think he recognized you in that getup."

"Hush, you." I realized I was still in my dress and brushed off any dirt that had gotten on the skirt. I might not like dresses, but I couldn't help feeling a bit bad ruining it so fast.

Gabriel and Cor finished talking, and Cor made a fake grin—the one he used to give to our parents when he was up to trouble. "Well then, shall I show you to our room? Then we can... catch up, I suppose."

"You could call it that."

Cor eyed me. "Please at least try to listen to me before you use that weapon that is under your skirt."

I narrowed my eyes. "How did you know I had a gun?"

"Because it's you we are talking about." He cocked a grin. "And because I know your frame quite well, Ellie."

Zach grabbed both my wrists before I could punch Cor again. Cor laughed as Gabriel glanced back and forth between Cor and me. He raised an eyebrow.

"So you two used to be an item?" Gabriel asked out of nowhere.

Zach looked away as I glared at Cor but at the same time wanted to slap Gabriel for asking about such things. This clearly wasn't the time or place.

The side of Cor's lip rose in a cocky grin. "Sure were. First loves to be exact."

Whatever concern and fear he had shown moments before was gone. I clenched my fist, calming myself down so I wouldn't make a scene. That was before he betrayed all our kind. How could he act so nonchalant about this? How could he seem like he was just the same old Cor whom I grew up with? Cracking jokes, making girls swoon with that cocky smile, having no cares in the world. It just wasn't fair. He was living it up with this guy with money while Zach and I had to make do with whatever spare job we could find. He destroyed our friends—our families—our lives.

Taking a deep breath, I peered over at Zach, who seemed as confused about all this. I wanted more than anything to go back to how things were, but it just wasn't in the cards. No, we were far from that ever happening. But apparently Cor thought acting like his old self was the only way to deal with stress. The more I thought about it, the more I realized it wasn't that surprising. He was trying to deal with it all just like we were.

The casino was quiet but quite grand—grander than anything I had ever been to. There were floating chandeliers dancing to the music that still played, even this early in the morning. Most of the betting tables were empty, but a few men and women of different races were playing either a very late game or a very early one. Everything was a shade of blue, but then I realized that was because I was still wearing the glasses Gabriel bought for me.

We made it up the stairs and into the master suite that Cor had. I glanced around. There were in fact two bedrooms in their suite. I was surprised by this, mainly because it was apparent that they shared a bed. Perhaps it was for guests, and all those rich people had more than one bed. Cor closed the door behind us, and I turned and punched him straight in the nose again. He slammed backward and hit his head on the door. He clutched both his bloody nose and the bruise forming in the back of his skull.

"Was that necessary?" he asked as he slid down the wall.

"Yes, it was!" I spat down at him.

"Hey, wait a minute!" Gabriel began when Zach

snatched him.

"Best you let her finish. We have a bit of pent-up rage. Don't worry. She won't kill him. Yet."

"But you claimed you all were friends who wanted to find him—you said you would listen to him."

I bent down and clutched Cor by the collar. "Oh, we were friends. That was until this bastard abandoned us and destroyed our home." Tears were rolling down my cheeks again. It had been three years since I had cried so hard. "And then, without an explanation, he disappeared!"

Cor peered up at me, sorrow in his eyes. That didn't mean I would forgive him. Nothing he could say or do would make me forgive him. He gave a shrug.

"Then do it. Kill me like you want to. Then I can be done with this guilt."

I shook my head. "No, you don't get to get off that easy. Gabriel is right—I deserve an explanation. Zach deserves an explanation. All those that you killed deserve an explanation! Now talk!"

Cor hesitated, as if he wanted more than anything to escape and ignore this conversation. It appeared he'd rather die than tell the truth. He glanced over at Zach, then sighed.

"Fine, but can we order some room service and chat over breakfast? It's going to be a long story."

CHAPTER XXII

<u>Zach</u>

It was half an hour before room service brought up our breakfast. As we all waited, I unpacked our things as I had a feeling we would be there for a bit. Ellie stayed in the main area and glared at Cor as he sat on the couch, both not saying a word. Gabriel took a shower, more than likely to get away from this awkwardness. I didn't blame him.

I didn't know what to make of the situation. We had been hunting Cor for so long, and everything we had done, good and bad, was for this moment. Now that we were here, however, I didn't know how I felt. Seeing Cor's face again made me realize we had been best of friends—we did everything together. Could I really go through with helping murder him? And was that still our plan?

He had led to the death of all our friends and family, that much was clear. He didn't deny it but said he was going to try to explain it all. That, in our line of work, indicated he was guilty. Although pleading innocent meant they were really guilty and didn't feel sorry for what they had done. Waiting to give a full explanation meant he did feel guilt. However, that didn't mean he was off the hook.

As I put away the last dress Gabriel had purchased for Ellie in our room, I sighed. I had a feeling she was experiencing the same thoughts as I was. He was guilty, yes, but deep down somewhere we still cared for our friend. And it made it all that much worse.

The spare room that Gabriel and Cor had was quite large—bigger than any room I had ever had. I ran my hand over the soft goose-feather-filled comforter. I couldn't wait to test this bed out—by sleeping in it of course. And it was king-sized, so Ellie wouldn't kick me all night. Well, hopefully.

Not able to wait any longer, I sat on the bed just to test out the springiness. Just as I had thought, it was soft and magnificent. I wanted to lie down right now as we didn't get much sleep on the ship. Perhaps after the talk we would get to. Exhaling a long breath, I got back up and went to see if food had been delivered yet.

As I stepped back into the main area, I found Cor and Ellie where I had left them. Before I could kill the awkward silence, there was a knock at the door, which made each of us jump and reach for our guns. Cor got up, his hand still on his gun, and peered out the peephole. I raised an eyebrow to Ellie, curious why he was so cautious, as he slowly opened the door.

A waiter, who was a human male about our age with blond hair, rolled in a cart that was full of plates covered with silver domes. He moved them onto the main dining table. Ellie didn't say a word as a plate was set in front of her. The man took off the domes, and steaming eggs, bacon, and hash browns covered each plate.

"Enjoy!" he said as he wheeled the empty cart out of the room.

I called after him. "Thank you!"

The door shut, and I glanced over to Cor. "You seemed a bit jumpy there. You used to someone not so innocent knocking on the door?"

"I'll get to that. But now food."

"And an explanation," Ellie added as she munched on a piece of bacon. "You promised one when we got food."

"You are as patient as ever, I see. I'll get to it; just give me a second."

"You've had twenty minutes. Now spill." Ellie glared at him over her glass of orange juice as she took a sip. There was no denying we were hungry and hadn't had this delicious of a breakfast in a while. Even though the food in the Lyran Zone was good, it wasn't this outstanding.

Cor took a seat as Gabriel came into the room. He saw the food and smiled as he pulled out his chair. "Finally, a yummy meal!"

I sat down next to Ellie and patted her leg. Her gaze didn't leave Cor.

As he took a bite of his eggs, he began the tale. "It started a couple of years before the destruction of Kaus. A human who went by the name of Obi offered to pay for my education at an elite school. He said first, though, he would have to teach me the basics since Kausians didn't even get that in our schooling, if any of us went to school."

I smiled a little as I recalled all the times we'd skipped class. It was sad, but it was our way of life. And besides, the schooling wasn't very great. Most of what we needed to learn we learned on our own anyway.

Ellie frowned. "So that was what you were up to all those times you disappeared randomly? Schooling?"

He nodded. "Yup. I was hoping to eventually bring you two with me, but Obi would never agree with it. For some reason, he wanted to only teach me, and I couldn't say no... I figured I could teach you once I had learned enough.

"Time passed, and I was ready to be tested to enroll in the school when Obi requested to come to Kaus. He said he wanted to speak to my parents to make sure everyone would be fine for school. I didn't know what to do. I was..." Cor looked down at his food as if the day was still fresh in his mind. I know it was fresh for us. "I was going to decline when other people showed up to Obi's home. They were all part of the elite group. There were Silurians and... And I knew it was something more."

"And yet you gave him the codes to get into Kaus," Ellie exclaimed as she drove the silver knife into the wooden table. The action even made me jump. Three years of emotions were swirling up inside her—I couldn't blame her for any of her random outbursts. I took her hand and squeezed it, letting her know it would be okay.

"I didn't have a choice! They were going to kill me if I said anything! I didn't think… I didn't think they were going to destroy everything! I figured…"

Ellie stood up, ripping her hand away from mine. "You figured what? That they were just going to come inside for a picnic?"

"I figured… I figured they would just take over. I didn't think they would destroy… I didn't think they would kill…" Cor blinked away tears. "I wouldn't have given them the codes if I'd known they were going to commit genocide."

I couldn't believe Cor was on the verge of crying. I had never seen him cry—not once. Not when his dad died, not when his younger sister got the illness and passed away at the age of five—not even when Ellie accidentally kicked him in the balls when we were seven years old. He really did feel guilty, which he was because he gave them the codes.

Leaning back, I pondered what I would have done in his situation. I had to admit if someone tried to become close to me and help, I would have figured they weren't going to kill everyone like that. But with the Silurians there, he should have known nothing good was going to happen. Glancing over to Ellie, who had sat back down, I could tell that she was thinking the same thing. Call it intuition or the fact that the two of us hadn't been apart for more than an hour in the past three years.

"Where is the human who betrayed you?" Ellie asked. "Did you kill him?"

Cor ate some more of his food. "No. I doubt he was really the mastermind. My focus has been on the Silurian who was there since it was them who destroyed our zone."

"Did you kill him then?"

He shook his head. "No. I have gotten close to him, however. It took some time to get him to trust me, and more time to get Gabriel into the society so I could enact my revenge."

"Which is what?" Ellie asked. "What could you possibly do other than murder him?"

Cor bit his lip. "Death is too easy. He wouldn't feel the pain that I have—that we have—endured. I want him to feel the worst pain of all."

"Which is what, exactly?" I asked.

He shrugged. "You will see."

I didn't know what to make of that. Was he going to destroy this Silurian's family? Was he going to massacre them in front of him or something? I would press him later, after I was thinking straight and could process everything that had happened in the past hour. I glanced at Ellie and found she was keeping her lips closed as well. She must have felt the same.

Cor finished his plate of food and wiped away any mess he had on his mouth and cheeks.

"Now, I don't know about you guys, but I'm tired. I worked all night, you traveled all night, and I think we need some rest. As for what to do while you're on this moon, well, we will figure that out once we wake up."

I glanced over to Ellie, who still was frowning. She finished her own plate of food. "How do you know I won't kill you in your sleep?"

Cor stood up. "Because you have had a gun pointed at me this entire time and haven't shot me. You're curious, just as always."

Leaning back, I spotted the gun. I hadn't even noticed. "What about the waiter? You seemed hesitant to let him in. What was that all about?"

Cor sighed. "We've had some issues with people wanting to murder Gabriel. Something about him not fitting in."

Gabriel smiled innocently. "I'm just too popular."

That made sense, as the two of us had also been hired to kill him. It was good to know that Cor was watching his back just as much as we were. That meant together we wouldn't miss a thing.

"I have one last question," Ellie said as she got up. "Why didn't you ever tell us the truth? First about the tutoring and then what had transpired... We could have ended this a long time ago if we'd put our heads together."

Cor stepped up to her and put his hand on her cheek. "Because you deserve better. You deserved a life better than anything I could have ever given you. It was why I went to the tutoring..." He shook his head and turned away. "It doesn't matter. Not anymore anyway. Good night, both of you. It's nice to know you two have survived all this."

With that, he went into his bedroom. Gabriel

followed after and shut the door.

Ellie had a single tear slowly fall down her cheek. She wiped it away and headed toward our room. I didn't say a word as I went with her, understanding it all now.

Cor had wanted to get the best education so he could provide for Ellie. It was a blow straight into the heart and stomach. There was nothing any of us could do now about it, and we had to just move on.

But we wouldn't. Because people like us never did.

CHAPTER XXIII

<u>Gabe</u>

I had never seen him like this. Cor was lying on the bed, curled up on his side. I sat down on the edge, watching him. His eyes were shut, and he was frowning.

"Are you going to sleep in your clothes?" I asked. At least he had taken his shoes off.

"I just… I just need a moment, all right?"

I nodded. That made sense after everything that happened and what he revealed. I had no idea he had gone through all that. Although I knew about his home being destroyed, I didn't know he had a part in it all. I couldn't imagine. He had been tricked, and because of that, his whole world was gone.

And he had been dealing with this for three years without even mentioning it.

I understood not wanting to bring it up. It was a big secret—a secret that most wouldn't have accepted. It was for a selfless reason, however, why he trusted such a shady person. He wanted to make a life with Ellie— he wanted to go to a nice university and get a good job. Now, instead of that promise, he was without a home, without a family, and was making his money through prostitution and gambling.

Was it bad that I pitied my own boyfriend?

One thing did occur to me, however, was the fact the woman in the other room wasn't just some ex, but was one he wanted to spend the rest of his life with. It wasn't because they had a falling out that they split up, but because he ran away.

Which meant he still cared for her.

At least that was what I thought. Perhaps I was wrong—perhaps he no longer felt anything for her. But the way he looked at her when she broke down in the middle of the spaceport painted a different story. It painted a story of two lovers who never got any closure.

And then there was the matter of the ring he always had in his pocket.

Was that the ring the two of them shared? Did she have one as well? It wasn't as if I could easily ask, but I had noticed there was a leather string that hung under her blouse. Perhaps that was what was on the other end of it.

So where did that leave me?

I didn't doubt Cor's feelings for me, but I didn't know if this woman meant something to him more. If so, was he going to leave me for her? The two of us had an open relationship, and I thought that was fine, but it was now occurring to me that our open relationship never had to do with loving someone else. It only had to do with sex.

"You know that I love you, right?" I said, more to reassure myself than him. "And I will accept you as you are."

Cor still didn't open his eyes. "Yeah, I know. I love you too, Gabe. I am glad I found you. I don't know what I would have done if you didn't come around and save my sorry ass."

It made more sense to me now as to why he was out there that day. He was trying to make it all end—he didn't care if he was saved or not. He had given up all hope. I had been in the same situation before—I could understand where he was coming from. Perhaps that was why I stopped the horse and helped him. I knew what it was like to want to die.

I let out a breath and smiled. "Well, I'm glad I saved you. You have been one hell of a boyfriend."

"So have you." Cor blinked his eyes opened. I noticed in the faint light coming from the crack in the blind that his eyes were red.

I wanted to wrap my arms around him and tell him everything would be all right, but I had a feeling he wanted his space, mainly because that was what he already said. I patted his leg and got up to change into my pajamas. There was no way I was going to bed in my new suit.

As I began to undress, Cor commented. "By the way, I like the new hat. Very cute."

I smiled. Perhaps I still had a chance.

CHAPTER XXIV

Ellie

I sat on the edge, rocking back and forth. Had that been true? Had Cor risked everything for me?

He didn't know what that man was planning—he had thought he was going to be let into a university. Then they threatened him and made him tell them the codes. Most Kausians didn't know the codes—Cor only did because his parents oversaw the shield.

Which meant they were targeting him on purpose.

I wanted to scream—I wanted to cry—I wanted to

tear and destroy everything around me. All this was because Cor wanted to make a life with me—a better life without sorrow, like all our friends and family.

The problem was I would have been happy no matter where we were as long as we were together. But that didn't happen—what happened was he left without saying a word. And for that, I didn't know if I could forgive him.

"Ellie, are you all right?" Zach stepped into the room and closed the door behind himself.

"What do you think?"

"You are right. It was a stupid question. I more meant, do you want to talk about it?"

I shrugged as he sat next to me and wrapped his arms around me. I leaned my head onto his chest as tears dripped from my eyes.

"I don't know what do, Zach—I don't even know what to think."

"I agree. It's a lot to process. We have been searching for him for so long—believing he did all this on purpose only to find he had been tricked."

I bit my lip. "It's not just that though, Zach. He was in that situation for me. He wanted to go to school and get an education for me."

He rubbed my back. "Don't you dare feel guilty about someone else's choice, you hear me? He didn't have to run after—he could have come to us."

If I were in his shoes, would I have done the same? Would I have run or would I have asked for their help? I wasn't sure—we were young then. It had only been three years, but I felt much older after everything we had to do—after everything we had to suffer through. But could I have admitted my mistake and lived with those consequences?

Zach squeezed me tighter. "I think we should get some rest and have a clearer head in the morning. Then from there we can figure out what to do. We are stuck on this moon—we might as well make the most of it. Not every day you get to be inside the society like this."

I laughed a little, but it was half-hearted. "Yeah, with every turn we could be killed right on the spot."

"You always did like a challenge." Zach kissed my head and held me a bit longer. I couldn't imagine my life without Zach—he was my better half, so to speak. He kept me levelheaded, which wasn't an easy task. Zach was there when it all happened, and he had to gather me up when I thought my life was no longer worth living. But now, with this new information, was I going to forgive Cor for what he did? Or would I find he was lying and have to finally pull the trigger?

There was only one way to find out.

CHAPTER XXV

<u>Cor</u>

I couldn't sleep.

I figured I wouldn't be able to, given everything that had happened in the past couple of hours. Why did they have to show up? It was the worst timing in the history of timing. Or at least a close second.

Turning, I found Gabe was out like a light. Of course he would be. He didn't quite comprehend what happened back then. He was a human—he wasn't a Kausian who always felt the fresh wound that was their city being destroyed. No matter how much time passed, it would always be fresh until the day we all died.

But that wasn't the biggest problem at the moment. Ellie and Zach were wanted by the Silurian government for gods only knew what. Supposedly, it was because they murdered a few back at a bar, but that seemed unlikely. Although I knew they were bounty hunters, I doubted they would kill unless it was part of the job or in self-defense. So there was more to the story.

I thought about coming clean about getting hired to kill them, but I figured that would add to the fuel of Ellie wanting to kill me. I wasn't going to do it, of course, but I needed time to think of how I would succeed in making Krax think they were dead. Only then would he give me the codes and let me into the Silurian Zone.

Then I would do exactly what he had done to my people.

I would make sure he wasn't around so that he could feel the same despair that I did. It had taken years for him to trust me and get to this place. I had betrayed people, done horrific things. But it would be worth it to see the look on his face when he watched all his friends and family go up in flames.

It was a dark plan—one that no one should think of, but this was about revenge. I didn't want to harm innocent people, but it was the only way. I doubted Ellie and Zach would agree to such a horrifying plan, but then again, they had come all this way and had killed just to find me.

To be honest, I was surprised Ellie didn't shoot me the moment she saw me. I would have if I were in her shoes. Perhaps she wanted to understand why I did what I did. Perhaps she thought there was still good in me. I doubted if there was—so much had happened in the past few years that I couldn't go back to being the person I used to be with her.

There was a strange pain in my chest. It had started the moment my eyes saw Ellie. Something inside me remembered the teenage girl with beautiful brown hair who used to hold my hand when we walked around Kaus and sneaked outside the city to find food and money. Her yellow eyes that were just a bit more golden than most other girls and boys—the same eyes I thought about as I studied hard to pass the exams to get into the Human Zone University.

Then they were the eyes that watched her own home get destroyed.

It had all been for nothing. My wish—my goals— were what led to the destruction of our kind.

It definitely wasn't Ellie's fault. No, it was all my own fault. But I couldn't face her after what had happened, and I ran away without a second thought. Now seeing her again—seeing how beautiful she was— I couldn't help but wonder what life could have been like if Obi hadn't betrayed me and had really meant to send me to school.

Okay, so maybe I still had feelings for her, and perhaps I thought of her more often than I liked to admit, but she would never see me like that again. The way she glared at me as if she wanted to see a hole through my head made that clear. No, our time had passed, and I needed to stop thinking about her. I needed to stop losing myself as I stared at the ring I had kept on my person at all times.

Gabe moaned in his sleep, bringing me back to the present. Then there was Gabe. I cared about him a lot— cherished the past two years we had spent together— but he and I were a lot alike, not to mention we had an open relationship. These thoughts of Ellie weren't betraying him, especially since I had known Ellie my entire life. Ellie and I had been best friends throughout our childhood and started dating in our teens. We had only ever loved each other at the time. Between her, Zach, and me, we didn't have any other friends. That was mainly because Zach was half human and no one wanted to befriend a family they thought betrayed our kind. So Ellie and I became his friend and thought the rest to be assholes, to be quite honest.

I had been quick enough to get the two of them out of Kaus. At least I had that going for me.

The pain in my chest turned into pain in my stomach. I was a piece of shit for letting everything that had happened happen, and nothing would remedy that. As sleep finally started to take over, I prayed to the gods that Ellie or Zach would come in here and finally end it all for me.

When I woke, I found my wish hadn't come true. I was still alive and still suffering with all the guilt. I stared up at the ceiling, which was a dark blue, and felt one tear slip out of the corner of my eye. I wiped it away and got in the shower before Gabe woke up. I listened carefully but didn't hear Ellie or Zach. Odds were I had only slept for a few minutes as my body didn't want to give me the pleasure of rest when there was so much to be done. I couldn't blame my body—I didn't deserve it.

The bathroom and shower were quite large. All this luxury was disgusting when my people didn't even have enough food, access to anything outside Kaus, or at least nothing they preferred. They feared us, and therefore they cut us off. Luckily we had community gardens and helped each other out, even those who married humans. Humans were a little more open to marrying our kind, but none of the others even gave it a thought. We had a river that went through the outskirts of town that luckily no one else poisoned. They realized they would be hurting themselves as well if they ever did such a thing.

I cleaned off and got out to find Gabe getting up. He still appeared tired, and I was surprised he could sleep so much with everything going on.

"Oh, you're up already?" Gabe asked. "Did you get any sleep?"

I shook my head. "No, but that's fine. I usually don't." I kissed the side of his head. "Get ready. I'm sure you will have a lot to do today. Talking to rich people and all that."

He nodded. "Right. I guess they would want me to be clean and tidy."

I smiled. "Exactly. It's already past lunchtime, so a lot of them are already downstairs mingling."

"Work, work, work," Gabe mumbled as he went into the bathroom, taking off his shirt. My eyes lingered on him until I realized I needed to check up on the other two.

I went into the main area to find no one there. I let out a breath as I went to their door and opened it. As soon as I started to enter, a pillow hit me straight in the face.

"Who gave you permission to come in here?" Ellie yelled as she folded her arms over her bra.

I picked up the pillow off the floor. "Well, technically it's my room in this hotel, so I give myself permission."

"Well, you can leave!" Her face was turning red. I knew I should have left her to change, but getting Ellie embarrassed and worked up used to be my favorite pastime. Perhaps it still was.

"Do you need help picking something out? Because seeing how you looked yesterday, not to mention the pants and dirty shirt you normally wear, I doubt you are capable of picking out your own clothes for a shindig like this."

Ellie pursed her lips. "How would you know what I

normally wear?"

"Well, because that is what you used to wear, and believe it or not, we have crossed paths a few times these last three years, but I'm like a sly fox and was able to escape before you found me."

"Damn you, Cor."

I tossed the pillow back on the bed and stepped closer to her. "Now please let me help."

She rolled her eyes but didn't bother arguing. I was surprised she didn't argue some more, and to be honest, I was hoping she would.

"So what did Gabe buy for you on the train?" I asked as I followed her to the wardrobe.

She gestured to the dresses. "It's all here. I don't know what to do with it, so have at it."

I flipped through the dresses, blouses, and skirts. He'd stuck with dark and bold colors, which matched her personality better than pastels. Even the brief time Gabe was with her, he understood that about her at least.

Ellie stayed next to me—oblivious she was still in her underwear. It wasn't as if I hadn't seen her naked before, but I was surprised she hadn't grabbed a robe or something as there were plenty in the bathroom. It was apparent she had just showered as her hair was wet and up in a towel still. I tried my best not to let my eyes linger on her exposed skin, not only because she was beautiful, but because she was covered in quite a few scars from what I could imagine were bullet and knife wounds.

I turned my attention back to the wardrobe. "I would go with that black blouse and dark green skirt. Some green-tinted glasses with it won't look too bad to hide your eyes. Then we can do your hair up all nice, put on some makeup, and no one will recognize you."

She shot me a look. "Why would you expect anyone to recognize me?"

"I mean... Well, aren't there people looking for you? You two seemed jumpy as well when the door rang this morning. And Gabe mentioned that you had to leave early because of some trouble."

Ellie narrowed her eyes for a moment, then nodded. "Yeah, seems some Silurians are after us. Typical. They hate our kind."

"That's a fact. Now put some clothes on so I can do your hair."

She let out a laugh. "What, are you some expert on doing women's hair now?"

I gave her a smug look. "In fact, I am. I do client's hair all the time. After I'm done with them, they usually need to fix their hair and makeup."

Her cheeks turned a bright red. "So what Gabe said was true—you're a prostitute."

"Prostitution and bounty hunting are the only accepted lines of work people like us can do. Lucky for you, I'm skilled at both."

She rolled her eyes, but I saw a sliver of a smile. "Whatever."

With that, she put on her blouse and skirt, and I sat her down in front of the mirror. I pulled out the curling iron from the closet and began heating it up.

"I presume Gabe bought some makeup on the train?"

She nodded to luggage that hadn't been put away. "It's in there."

I opened up the luggage and grabbed the supplies Gabe had purchased. He seemed to have it all covered, which was surprising. He typically knew nothing of women's fashion sense.

I applied some foundation and blush and worked on her eye shadow and eyeliner.

"I'm surprised you aren't putting up more of a fuss."

"Well, I mean, I did when we bought it. Seems like a

waste of effort now."

"I meant being around me."

She was silent for a moment. "I wasn't able to sleep last night, thinking about what you said. I don't forgive you for what happened, but I'm not sure I can blame you either. I am mad that you left me and Zach to pick up the pieces—I'm mad that this all happened because you were trying to make us a better life. I just... I don't know what to feel, and I'm taking it one step at a time."

I knew that feeling. Part of me wanted things to go back to how they used to be between us—that was why I came in here and acted like I did and was now putting on her makeup for her. But I knew it was a lie—I knew it was just me trying to deal with my sins.

"As for you hating makeup, though, I think it's just a front. I think you secretly love it."

She tried to squirm, but I grabbed her jaw so she couldn't mess me up.

"No, not a front. I hate all this girly stuff. The only reason I agreed was that Gabe pointed out I could hide guns under a skirt easier."

That sounded so typical of Ellie that I had to hold back my laughter. But that also reminded me of something I wanted to talk to her about. "Speaking of which, I have an important assignment for you while you're here."

I finished putting her eye makeup on, and she raised a now-perfect eyebrow. "Oh, what is that?"

"I need you two to watch over Gabe while he is here. As you both know, there are a lot of people who want him dead. But do it in a way that's not obvious, and of course try not to show your face or eyes or let anyone know you exist."

"Oh, is that all?" She shook her head. "Sounds like a typical Tuesday."

Before I could delve further into what the rest of their days of the week were like, Zach stepped out of the bathroom in just his underwear. I glanced between the two of them. They seemed close. Really close.

"Are you two…," I began, feeling a little nudge of a jealous tug at my heart.

Both of them answered in unison. "Ew, no!"

I laughed. Some things never changed—they both answered in unison quickly. Perhaps they really were just best friends.

"Ellie, what are you letting him do to you?" Zach asked as he put on one of the suits that Gabe bought.

I held up the hair curler. "I'm styling her hair."

A smirk appeared on Zach's face. "Well, that's good. She doesn't know how to do that herself."

Ellie whipped her head around, and I almost burned her face with the iron. "Hey! Take that back!"

Zach shook his head. "It's true."

She pouted but didn't say anything. This really was like old times, and yet so much had changed. And so much was going to change once they knew the truth of what I wanted to do to the Silurians.

And for that, there would be no forgiveness.

CHAPTER XXVI

Ellie

I peered at myself in the mirror, still not sure how Cor was able to pull it off. I didn't even recognize myself. My face was clean and perfect like those girls at the fancy shindigs, and my hair was defying all laws of physics with how it was curled and pinned up in the back. The glasses made me look sophisticated but gentle in some weird way. And the blouse and skirt— well, I hated them. Skirts and dresses were stupid, and I would die on that hill.

Zach gave me a snicker as he saw the aggravation in my eyes as I peered down at my clothes. I shot him a look. "Don't give me that! Wearing a dress sucks! Especially if I'm supposed to be guarding someone."

"Hey, suits aren't that easy either. I feel constricted." He adjusted the vest, but it didn't seem to do him any good.

"How about I kick you in the face?"

"Which you could do because you're less constricted."

The door from our bedroom to the main area was open, and I didn't see any sign of Cor or Gabriel. They were probably finishing getting ready as were we. I went over and closed the door so I could talk to Zach without being heard.

"So what do you think?"

Zach sat down on the edge of the bed. "About which part? About how we are up here on Zynon, how we found Cor, what Cor said, or the fact that he's really good at doing a lady's hair and makeup?"

"Well, all of it if I'm honest. I mean, look at my face. I don't recognize my face."

"Neither do I. If you passed me by on the street, I wouldn't have known it was you."

"Right?" I sighed as I started to pace around the room. "But truthfully, Zach, what should we do?"

He shook his head. "I honestly don't know. This isn't the scenario I thought we would find ourselves in when we located Cor. I figured he would be out doing something wicked so we could just not feel bad about killing him. But now, with everything he said, I don't know."

I started to scratch at my forehead when I realized I was ruining the powder Cor put down. "Shit, is it fine?"

"Can't tell you fucked with it, no."

"Good." I let out a sigh. "I'm just... I'm torn. I feel guilty, Zach. I mean, he was... He was doing it all for me. He wanted to provide for me and then... well..."

Zach stood up and wrapped his arms around me. "None of this was your fault. You didn't have any role to play. It was the bad people who tricked Cor. I think we should help him finish this mission and enact his revenge. Perhaps once we find out who was behind it all, we can verify the story or something. I don't know. Let's just... Let's just see how this plays out."

I nodded my head as he squeezed me tight. Luckily, I couldn't feel any more tears, as if I had cried them all earlier. Otherwise, I would have completely ruined my makeup. But the truth was, now that I was here, all those feelings for Cor I thought I had forgotten were coming back. I didn't think they still existed—I didn't think it was possible. Except they were there, and now I would have to face them.

Stepping away from Zach, I grabbed the ring I always wore and stuck it in my purse for safekeeping. "Well, let's get going, shall we?"

The two of us stepped out into the main area of the suite and found Cor and Gabe were waiting for us. Cor was wearing an all-black suit with dark spectacles that made his white hair seem even brighter. I had always loved his hair—it was unique since most Kausians were either blond or brunette.

"Well, what is on the agenda today?" Zach asked. "Rich-people things? Like smoking expensive foul-smelling cigars, drinking gross amber alcohol, and wasting money as if it were tissues?"

Cor pondered on that thought. "Yeah, pretty much."

I pounded my fist up in the air. "Yay whiskey! And smokes!"

Zach let out a sigh as he knew I was going to partake in such devices. I gave him the biggest smile.

Cor gave us a soft smile. I wasn't sure what that was

about, but I tried to turn my attention on Gabriel. "Well, Gabriel, are you ready for another day with the two of us?"

He nodded. "Can't be too bad. Better than you two trying to kill me. We will have to try to stay discreet though. We won't want to catch people's attention."

I raised an eyebrow. "You're the one who clearly has the attention of people who want you dead. I think Zach and I will be fine."

He clapped his hands together. "Right. Well, just don't show your eyes."

Zach added to the conversation. "And don't whore us out. We aren't Cor."

"I'll try to remember. I just hope you're both good at poker."

"I'm better at blackjack, to be honest," I commented as I glanced at Cor. He was the one who had taught me how to count cards. "But I'm not bad."

"Good. We will need that when we enter the tournament in a couple of days. If one of us wins, we will be set for life. Also, you can call me Gabe from now on. A friend of Cor's is a friend of mine."

I didn't feel that Gabe quite understood everything that went on. He wasn't part of the plot to get revenge, I realized. Cor was using him to get close to Krax. I wondered how much of their relationship was a lie and how much of it was real. Or perhaps it was mutual agreement.

I grinned. "I think between Cor, Zach, and I, we can wipe the floor with everyone. It was how we made money growing up, after all."

Cor grinned. "That it was. Now, should we go get some practice in?"

I nodded as we headed out into the corridor, but not before I swiped a key card that was lying on the table. There was no way I was going to leave this room without having access to it, even if none of my actual belongings were in there. If the opportunity presented itself, then I could search around and see if I could find any info about what was really going on in Cor's head.

It didn't seem Cor had noticed as he was searching around for anyone who could come out and attack us, which wasn't reassuring. Zach and I joined him, as we were also used to having to watch our backs. Gabe clearly wasn't. It was how we were almost able to assassinate him so easily. How he managed to survive this long was quite a miracle.

It was something I had noticed earlier—Gabe didn't

seem like he wanted to go unnoticed. He wanted to be a damsel in distress, so to speak. I wasn't sure why that was. I was far from a person who could read others. But it did make me curious.

He was wearing a new suit today, but he had on his green hat from before. The suit was all gray that paired quite well to the vibrant green hat. I wondered if he was the one who taught Cor to be fashionable, or if it was the other way around. It didn't matter in the long run, but I wanted to know how Cor had changed in the past three years and what led to those changes.

We rounded corners, and I did my best not to trip on my skirt. I hiked it up a bit and knew it was improper for me, but I couldn't help it. Wearing a dress sucked.

"Ellie, you stand out a bit, walking around like that. Be more ladylike," Zach said, teasing me, although we both knew there was some truth to his comment.

"I'm adding teach Ellie to be more ladylike to my mental to-do list." Cor sighed. "I mean, I knew we grew up in a rough place, but honestly, Ellie."

I stuck my tongue out at him. "Didn't see you complaining when we were younger."

A smile escaped his lips. "I didn't say I didn't like it, but you would think you would at least learn the basics to fit in."

"Whatever. I never have had to. Typically, I just gun someone down or attack them. I rarely seduce, but when I do, usually it works."

"Well, luck does happen," Cor commented under his breath. I shot him a look as Zach started laughing.

We made our way into the elevator and went down to the main level that had to be the main hall. It had a few tables of poker, blackjack, and every other game I could think of. People of all different races sat at the tables, other than Kausian, of course. No, they didn't exist as far as most of these people were concerned. Most thought we were a myth, which was just stupid and racist. Genocide happened to our people, and yet everyone forgot about it. Or perhaps they just didn't care.

"This is the only floor that has both some games and food," Cor explained. "The other floors are segregated between what games you want to play and then the hotel section by what race you are, and the top floor is the fine dining. I figured being down here, with everything that is going one, we will be less likely to stand out."

That made sense. Zach and I nodded as we inspected

the area. He was right. Everyone seemed busy between the gambling and the food. No one was looking at us.

"Keep your eye out for Byron and any Silurian," Zach whispered. "We should probably stay away from them the most."

I replied, "Already on it."

Silurians held grudges, and if they realized we were on this moon base, they would stop at nothing to kill us. I couldn't say I exactly wanted to die that day, so I would definitely be staying away from them.

I turned to Gabe. "Well then, Gabe, where do you want to start?"

He took a deep breath. "Well, I am a bit peckish. How about some food over there and sit at the blackjack table?"

"Can't say no to blackjack, and I could eat. I believe it's past lunch now."

Zach grabbed his stomach. "That it is. My stomach keeps telling me things."

Cor stepped back. "You three get food. I have some important things to discuss with a few people."

I didn't like where that was going. Did he really just want us to chaperone his boyfriend while he went off doing whatever he wanted? I knew he wanted us to protect Gabe, but after watching how Gabe acted in public, without a worry in the world, I realized this was going to be a harder job than I originally thought—not to mention I wanted to know where Cor was heading off to. Although I was beginning to believe he wasn't directly responsible for betraying Kaus, I still didn't trust him. What if it all had been a lie? What if he was setting us up? If that were the case, however, he'd had his chances to take us out. But then what would these meetings be about? What extra webs had he weaved that he didn't tell us about?

Cor left us, and we headed toward the buffet area. I leaned in to whisper into Zach's ear. "Should we follow him?"

"My brain says yes, but my stomach says no."

I rolled my eyes and glanced in the direction that Cor had left, which was back toward the elevator. I thought about going after him, but we all agreed we needed to be more discreet than that. I also didn't know this area well and wouldn't be able to sneak around in this dress. Then again, no one would think a woman was causing trouble. If anyone asked, I could just say I was lost and looking for the bathroom.

"I'm going to follow him. Keep an eye on Gabe."

"Will do. Don't get caught."

"I won't. At least probably. Hopefully. I'll try my hardest not to."

"That's reassuring."

I lifted my dress a little and hurried back to where the elevators were. If I was quick enough, I would be able to see which floor it stopped at so I would have a sense of where he was. As I got to the elevators, I saw a light blink. He was on the ninth floor. I pressed the button, and an elevator to the left opened up. I quickly pressed number nine and grabbed on to the railing as it begun to go up.

I hated elevators. I didn't hate them as much as I hated spaceships, but they were definitely one of the worst things in the world. Give me stairs any day— except while wearing a dress, of course.

The elevator dinged as it opened, and my eyes widened as I found a handful of Silurians staring at me. I smiled innocently.

"Sorry, wrong floor."

I jammed my finger on the Close Door button and felt my heart rate had doubled in a matter of seconds. What in the world was he doing on this floor? Had I been mistaken, or was there something else going on?

My finger lingered on the button to go back down to where Zach and Gabe were when I realized this would be as good a time as any to search Cor's bedroom for any hints of what he was really up to.

Deciding that was the best course of action, I headed back to our room and prayed Zach wouldn't start drinking while I was gone.

CHAPTER XXVII

Zach

"Wow, look at all this food." I stared at the buffet, wondering where to start. Cured meats, cheeses, fruits, grilled veggies, muffins, rolls—it was all there, waiting for me to eat it.

"Zynon definitely has the best food, I give it that," Gabe commented as he grabbed his own plate and began filling it.

I followed and piled as much as I could onto the plate, all of which I would eat, of course. I couldn't believe Ellie would leave this buffet table to follow Cor. She was an idiot. Although it would be waiting for her when she got back here, so I guess she wasn't too much of an idiot.

Saloons typically had free food for those who ordered drinks, but it was never this extravagant. It was meat, which one had to grab early before it began to spoil. Same went for the cheese and bread. This, on the other hand, appeared as if they rolled it out every hour and kept adding to it. I was going to stuff my face this entire mission. I wasn't ever going to want to go back home.

Gabe found us a table that currently no one was sitting at. The two of us took our seats, and I began to chow down as a waiter came over.

"Would you two like anything to drink?"

Before I could answer, Gabe ordered for me. "Two mimosas."

The waiter nodded and went to fetch the mimosas.

I turned to Gabe. "Should we really be drinking? We need to be alert if anyone comes after us."

He shrugged. "We would stand out if we didn't drink. Besides, Ellie should be back soon. What, did she go to the bathroom or something?"

"Or something, yeah." I took a bite of my food and

tried not to drool. It was better than I could ever imagine. I had never had food so exquisite as this. I just wished I could eat it every day. Although, I had to admit, some home cooking my mother used to make was better, even with the poor-quality ingredients we had. She always used to say with the right spices, she could make anything delicious.

"Is this really how rich people eat?" I asked as I stuffed my face.

Gabe nodded. "Yup. Meanwhile, people in every zone go hungry. Quite ridiculous, right? I mean, a lot of places have free food, but it isn't actually free unless you pay for drinks or some service. Normally Cor and I stay at hotels like that, although we do eat at nice casino such as this or a restaurant of some kind. I like eating at nice places, to be honest. I like making the people part of the society mad."

"Because you are half human, half Sirian?"

Gabe's eyes widened. "How did you…"

"The person who hired us told us. I'm also half human, so I get it. You want to prove to others you are worthy. Most don't know I'm half, however, since they already hate me for being a Kausian." I didn't want to complain more than that as I knew this guy had it hard as well. And I noticed how much he was fidgeting.

"I don't really talk about it, and not many can tell unless they already know. Cor... He doesn't even know, or at least he hasn't said anything. I would appreciate it if you didn't bring it up in front of him. I still need to tell him everything about my past, and I haven't yet."

Now that was interesting. He had a point—it was hard to tell if you didn't know. If he had surgery or dental work done, it definitely helped. However, I couldn't imagine why he wouldn't have had told Cor. It wasn't like he would have judged, but I supposed after being bullied and having people try to kill you for being what you were, I could understand that.

"My lips are sealed. And I will tell Ellie as well. Don't worry."

He smiled a little and went back to eating his food. "Thank you."

"It is ironic though. Neither you nor Cor knew each other's complete history or what is driving and you, but you both had the same goal. You just want to show the person who destroyed your life what's up."

"I suppose, in a way. It's probably why we were attracted to one another."

"And became boyfriends."

"Or something like that, yes. But he and Ellie used to be together, right?"

I slowly nodded. This took another awkward turn. I didn't know how to handle relationship talk, especially since I had never had to talk about relationships before, and this whole situation was rather complicated.

Gabe took a bite of the ham. "It's obvious they both care about each other still. I wonder if Cor ever realized she was still alive."

I shrugged. "It's not like we were very discreet in finding him. He had to have known we were coming after him."

"I suppose if he thought you were going to kill him, he wouldn't have let you close. It seemed like that was your plan, after all."

I held up my hands. "Hey, I just follow Ellie around and do what she wants. While I do want to see him pay, I also wanted to know the truth."

"So do you still think he is guilty?"

That was a good question. "I think, if he isn't lying, he was tricked. But that doesn't mean that he's not guilty. He just didn't think it would lead to the destruction of everything, but he knew they were going to attack or take over if he gave the codes. However, I don't know what I would have done in his shoes. I probably would have been too scared to think straight and perhaps would have given the codes as well. We were just teenagers at the time, after all."

"I suppose we never know what we would do in a situation, now do we?"

I shook my head. "No, I think we all have our own story for a reason. It's just how we learn from each decision and event that shows our true growth and character. It seems Cor is trying to fix what he has done, although there is no true way to fix it."

"There are definitely a lot of things in this world that can't be fixed. But we can die trying."

I understood that feeling all too well. We turned back to our food and stayed silent, not wanting to go back to the heavy conversation we were just having. After a few moments, our mimosas came, and we thanked the waiter. I took a sip and marveled at the sweetness of the orange juice mixed with expensive champagne. I had never had such delicate champagne before.

"I could drink a hundred of these," I said, flabbergasted.

Gabe laughed. "I know, right? They are a treat up here. Apparently, the oranges are grown upstairs in a greenhouse, and they must do something to make them sweeter than normal. As for the champagne, it is made by the Pleiadeans. It's the only thing we can get from their island, and only ships marked by the trading company are allowed in. It is the most expensive champagne, to say the least."

"I hadn't even realized the Pleiadeans made any contact outside their island. The more you know."

"It was rather recent. I'm not even sure how someone was able to contact them in the first place. Perhaps one traveled out to get supplies, and that was all he could sell."

That seemed the most likely. "Well, here is to the strange hermit race."

Gabe clinked his glass to mine. "Hear, hear."

I took a large sip and set the glass down. Even though I hadn't had much, I felt a little bit of a buzz already. It wasn't anything more food couldn't fix, however. I stood up.

"I am going to go get some more food. Need anything?"

Gabe shook his head. "Nope, I'm all good."

I went back to the buffet and filled my plate up with more cheeses, meats, potatoes, and anything that would fit. There was even some kind of goat cheese with blueberries in it. What will people think of next?

Realizing I shouldn't stay too enamored with the buffet and keep an eye on Gabe, I turned back to the table to find the worst situation imaginable. I almost dropped my plate—almost. I would have been really sad if I had, as I hated wasting food, but I doubted it would look good if I ate the food that fell on the floor. But never mind that—I had to deal with the situation at hand.

Byron was sitting at the table next to Gabe.

He made it up here faster than I thought he would. He must have gotten the note and money back and came up here to see if Gabe had already made it to Zynon. I noticed Gabe's expression. His eyes were wide, and I could see his hands shake. He knew the dangers that man brought with him.

"Crap on a cracker."

CHAPTER XXVIII

<u>**Gabe**</u>

He was already up here.

My entire body felt as if it were paralyzed. I thought I wouldn't be able to breathe ever again. I wanted to run —to hide—and never see his face again.

No good ever came from Byron.

"Well, if it isn't my favorite person in the entire world. Gabriel Pickett."

I tried to smile, but the muscles weren't responding. "Lord Byron Hill. What have I done to receive the pleasure of your company?"

"Oh, you know what you have done. You have existed, my dear Gabriel. No matter what I do, here you are. Alive and well."

I clinched my mimosa, debating if I should down it. It would make me feel better, but I couldn't give him the satisfaction.

"What can I say—I am a survivor."

Byron leaned in closer. "Is that so? I remember a scared little boy who wanted more than anything to disappear. What happened to him?"

"He woke up and saw the injustice of the world."

He leaned back and laughed. "Well, I'll be. You have grown a spine. I presume that is Cornelius's work. He has always been one to make people change. I hated that about him."

I narrowed my eyes. "How do you know Cor?"

"We go way back. I have known him for a long while now, but not as long as I have known you, of course. I have known you since the day you were born."

I hated Byron's smile. It wasn't that it was fake, but that it was devious—as if he could murder a child and take delight in it. I would know.

"Speaking of," he went on. "I just spoke to your

mother. She misses you terribly. You should go home sometime. I'm sure everyone there would be happy to see you."

He knew as well as I that was a lie. No one wanted me back home except my mother. They all hated me—they hated what I was. I had been called vile names, abused, threatened.

But it was Byron who twisted all their words. It was Byron who made them all hate me. He was the one who poisoned everyone's minds and made them think it was their own idea.

And that was why he was the most dangerous man on this moon.

Before I could respond, Zach came up to the table with his food.

Byron peered up at him with a devilish smile. "Well, hello there. I believe we have met before." He held out his hand. "Zachariah, wasn't it?"

Zach appeared almost white, but he did his best to smile—better than me, at least. "That it is. It's good to see you again, Lord Byron."

"Take a seat. I was talking to Gabriel here about how nice it will be to have another human in the club. There are a lot of Silurians, which can be rather unpleasant."

"Better not say that too loud," I commented. "They don't like humans that much already. They will take any chance they get to make another race shut up."

Byron laughed. "I like you, Gabriel. I think the two of us will have great fun this week. Now, where is that servant of yours? Or have you tossed him out and replaced him with this chap?"

"Nah, he had a meeting with someone. This here is one of his friends who agreed to be my bodyguard for the week. He has another partner too—a woman named Elvira. She is strong and not someone to piss off, to say the least."

Byron raised an eyebrow as he peered at Zach. "You don't say. Well, I hope he won't have to work too much. Then again, I've heard many people have it out for you, little Gabriel."

"Is that so? Well, I'm sure Zach will give them a good show."

Byron watched him closely, as if amused by the situation and by what I had said. I glanced over toward the elevators, wondering what could be taking Cor and Ellie so long. If this man tried anything, I wasn't all that sure Zach could take him.

"You know," Byron tapped his finger on the table.

"Zachariah, I happened to see your face somewhere. I believe it was on some wanted posters in the Lyran Zone. I wasn't too sure if it was you as you didn't seem like a hardened criminal. But the post had quite a handsome sum. All one needed to do was to report you to the nearest Silurian."

I froze. He wouldn't, would he? If I knew Byron, he hated Silurians with a passion. There was no way he would give them what they wanted, even if it meant hurting people who went back on their word.

Zach shrugged. "Must have been some other handsome redhead."

Byron laughed. "I suppose it was. Well, I better be off. A poker table is calling my name. I can hear it."

I turned and asked. "Will you be entering the poker tournament in a couple of days, Lord Byron?"

He nodded as he put on his top hat. "Indeed I am. I hope I'll see you there."

"Of course. Wouldn't miss it."

"Well then, I'll bid you farewell and good luck."

He left us sitting there, and I let out a breath I had been holding. I peered over at Zach, who was staring at his plate of food. It appeared as if he were debating if he was still hungry after that ordeal. After a moment, he began to eat. I was glad Byron didn't call over any Silurians.

"So you think he is mad that you went back on your word and didn't kill me?"

Zach nodded as he stuffed a pancake in his mouth. "Yup."

"Well, that is going to be fun to deal with. I need another round of mimosas."

"Should we? We probably need to be on high alert."

I shrugged. "I mean, if he were going to do something to us, he would have already done it. He is waiting—he's got a plan. Besides, Cor and Ellie should be back soon, shouldn't they?"

"They should. But she's going to get mad if I drink more than I have."

"Well, just eat more food, and it should be fine. Besides, how much alcohol does a mimosa have? Practically nothing."

Zach appeared to ponder on that thought. "You have a point—they aren't like martinis."

I patted his back. "Exactly. So I will be right back."

CHAPTER XXIX

<u>Cor</u>

I entered Krax's room, and the way he eyed me as I sat down across from him was not a good sign. There were other Silurians in the room, and I couldn't tell if they were the same as before as many reptilians appeared the same to me. They all wore the same clothing as well as they wanted to seem unified.

I took a deep breath and gave Krax my best smile. "Krax, you called for me? You usually don't call again so quickly after giving me a job. I saw you just last night. What's up?"

He clicked his long, hooked claw on the table. I had been scratched by Silurian claws—it was not an experience I wanted to repeat. Krax's nostrils flared as if he were trying to find the right words.

"Do you not have anything to tell me about your mission I gave you?"

I had to play innocent. I couldn't let him know the truth, or all this would be for nothing. "I don't have the faintest clue what you're talking about. The mission was to kill two Kausians. You know as well as I that no Kausians are up here. I will get to it once Gabriel is officially in the society."

"Quit the crap, Cornelius. I know they are here—I know they are staying with you. Explain to me what is going on."

How were they able to figure that out? Did Ellie draw too much attention yesterday? I was keeping an eye out —there weren't any Silurians around at the time. Since then, we had been in our room. There was no possible way he knew this information to be a fact—he was going off rumors.

I shrugged. "Sure, some human friends of Gabe came with him, but they aren't anyone you should worry about. They are just extra muscle to keep him safe."

He slammed his fist on the table, making me jump. "No, they aren't just some humans. Two of my men in the Human Zone were killed yesterday, but before they were murdered, I got word that two Kausians were with Gabriel. What are you hiding from me?"

Shit. Shit, shit, shit. I had to think this one through. I gave him another smile and held up my hands. "Look, I didn't know they were coming, but I do know Gabe's life is in danger due to many inside this organization. If you want them dead, fine. I'll kill them after the poker tournament and induction ceremony are finished. But meanwhile, they are his bodyguards. I can't be watching Gabe and juggling everything else by myself. I need them."

Krax brought his thick fingers into a steeple. "You think you're in a position to negotiate the rules?"

"I think they can benefit both of us. I think I can get my use out of them, and then after everything is done, you will get your wish. They won't cause trouble—I promise you that. And if they do, then I will kill them right then and there."

"What's in it for them? Why would they have agreed to keep Gabriel safe? How do I know they aren't planning to attack more of my men?"

I took a deep breath. "Gabe paid them handsomely. You know how Kausians are—they will do anything for money. Gabe saw them in action and hired them on the spot. You know how compulsive he can be. And since I have already had to kill two bounty hunters up here—in my own room, might I add?—I need all the extra help I can get."

Half of that was a complete and utter lie, but Krax didn't know why they had actually made their way up there. They wanted to kill me, or at least get their revenge, which actually involved Krax, but they didn't know that yet. This lie would work, however, as he thought all Kausians would sell their soul for a quick buck. This all wasn't that far of a stretch to him.

"Fine. But the moment you leave here, I better get a notice that they are dead, you hear me? They killed some important friends of mine in the Lyran Zone. I will not forgive them."

That's right. I forgot to ask them about that. I made a mental note to bring it up to Ellie or Zach. Neither of them seemed like they would kill without purpose. I wondered if it was self-defense or something else.

"Of course. Wouldn't have it any other way. Besides,

they aren't too keen on me. I have a feeling they want me dead as well."

"Well, you did betray your own kind. I can't blame them."

I took a slow, deep breath. I wanted to kill Krax right then and there, but that wouldn't do me any good. No, I had to enact my revenge a different way—I had to show him the pain of losing everyone. It was the only way I could repent—it was the only way for all my dead friends and family to get their vengeance in the underworld.

But either way, I needed to get out of there so I could calm down.

"Is that all, sir? I'm missing out on a good meal and some gambling."

He waved his hand. "You may leave. Just make sure you do as you're told next time. No more hiccups."

"Don't worry. No mission after this will have any problems."

Because there wouldn't be any more missions. I would have destroyed him.

I got up and left him sitting at his table. I didn't want to be around the man longer than I had to. I wanted him dead, and every moment made the itchy feeling worse. I ventured down the hallways, my stride quick as I ignored the Silurians who glared at me. I pushed up my glasses closer to my eyes. It wasn't as if everyone didn't already know I was Kausian as I had been dealing with these people for quite some time, but I couldn't help to be wary. At least there were humans who also liked the fashion statement, so I didn't stand out among them. But most of them were colored like the ones that Ellie and Zach wore. I work black, mainly because I didn't like the feeling of everything tinted one color. And because I felt black suited me. I was the bringer of death, after all. Or at least it felt like it.

I took the elevator back down to the lower level and searched for the others. It took a little bit, but I found Gabe and Zach sitting at a table, still eating, with about six mimosa glasses surrounding them. I pinched the bridge of my nose. How was he not dead from his stupid ideas and obliviousness? That was one thing that always got on my nerves about him. But his cuteness always made up for it.

I glanced around some more but saw no sign of Ellie. That was never a good sign—she was the worst about getting into trouble. I hurried to Gabe and Zach's table.

"Where's Ellie?" I was quick to ask.

Both Zach's and Gabe's faces were tinted a bit pink. Zach gave me a big grin. "Cor! You're back! I thought Ellie would be right behind you!"

I was going to have marks on my nose from where I kept pinching it. It was just one migraine after another. "And why would you say that?"

"Because she followed after you when you went off for your meeting or whatever," Zach slurred. He held up a mimosa that was still full. "Want a drink?"

Of course I did. I grabbed both Zach's and Gabe's drinks and downed them before they could get any more drunk. They both aahed in disappointment.

I set the glanced down. "Sober up. Drink some water and coffee. I'll be right back."

It was obvious that Ellie didn't make it on the Silurian floor—I would have seen her or the Silurians would have captured her and brought her to Krax. Once she saw where I was, she would have left. But since she wasn't downstairs, that meant she went up to our room to peek around. Ellie was persistent—I would give her that.

Then it hit me—I was used to hiding stuff from Gabe, not from Ellie. She was going to find those folders Krax had given me, and then she was going to kill me.

Shit.

CHAPTER XXX

Ellie

I nodded to the gentleman and lady who were boarding the elevator as I got off on the floor our bedroom was on. I did my best to make sure they didn't see my eyes. They too wore glasses, so Cor and Gabe were right about not standing out with them. I didn't like that everything was tinted green, however, but at least I would stay out of any unnecessary fistfights about what I was. Instead, I would just get into them the normal way—with my loud mouth.

I ventured down the hallway and took out the key card. It was clear that the richer folks were, the more gadgets they had. I had never seen a key card like this before as all the hotels I frequented used keys. Then there was the fact they were able to build a casino on the moon while hundreds upon hundreds struggled to find food. Didn't seem fair to me, but nothing in life had been fair as I struggled to stay alive.

Shaking my head, I scanned the key card on the pad, and the door beeped that it was unlocked. It opened, and I quickly got to work.

I doubted anyone would walk in on me, but one couldn't be too careful. I double-checked the rooms, not sure if someone had already sneaked in and was waiting or was like me and searching for something. It seemed Cor had as many enemies as we did, which was rather amusing. He had as many problems as Zach and I did.

Once I made sure it was clear, I went straight to Cor's bedroom and began snooping around. If he were going to hide something, I would assume he would hide it near where he slept. I checked under the mattress but found nothing there. I pulled out drawers and fumbled through the underwear, socks, and pants, but found nothing of interest. I sighed as I put it all back and closed the drawer. I wasn't tidy about it either. I didn't really care if Cor knew I went through his stuff—he deserved it.

I opened the closet and searched through suit pockets and anywhere someone could stick something. Other than guns and knives—a lot of them, to my surprise—I found nothing. I jammed a couple of the knives in my purse. One couldn't be too careful, and they weren't being used at the moment.

Next, I went through the bathroom cabinet. There were a couple of razors, toothbrushes, hair gel, and some herbs that I recognized to be male enhancers. I rolled my eyes as I shut the cabinet mirror. TMI.

So there was nothing in the bedroom or bathroom. That left the living area and the room Zach and I had slept in. While I doubted Cor would hide anything where we slept, he didn't know we were coming. So it was possible he hid whatever it was in there from Gabe but didn't know we would be in there.

If there was anything to hide, that is. For all I knew, Cor could have told us everything and wasn't lying, but if history taught me anything, it was Cor always had secrets. He couldn't help but lie. It was his nature.

I checked through the drawers of the desk in the

living room, feeling the bottom to make sure it wasn't fake and hiding something, but only found blank pieces of paper and pens. I went to the couch and lifted the cushion.

"Bingo," I said as I grabbed the two folders. Folders always meant business.

I placed them on the table and then began to flip through them when I frowned. They were about us— Zach and me. And the orders were to exterminate.

"Are you fucking kidding me? What is he up to?"

My heart was racing, and my mind struggled to keep up. Was he going to kill us? If that were the case, he'd had plenty of time to do so already. But these were definitely extermination papers. What was he doing with these? And who hired him?

Before I could put the folders away, the door to the hotel room swung open abruptly. Before I could grab my gun, I found Cor standing in the doorway, his gun at the ready.

Cor glanced at what I had found and let out a sigh. "I can explain."

I raised an eyebrow as he closed the door behind himself, his gun still pointing at me. "Oh, I can't wait to hear."

"I got those orders before you came up here. A few hours, in fact. You two have impeccable timing."

"Should I just go ahead and shoot you, Cor? Because right now I have an itch to not believe anything you say ever again."

He nodded. "I don't blame you, honestly. But I'm not going to kill you. If I wanted to, I would have done so while you slept."

"Fair enough, but then why are you still pointing the gun at me?"

"Well, because I know you will kill me if I lower it."

"That's true, but if you want me to trust you, lower your gun."

Cor hesitated, but he lowered the gun. I didn't make a move for mine as I knew there was more to the story. That, and he'd had his chance to kill me.

I folded my arms and sat down on the cushion I hadn't yet flipped. "So what was your plan? Make us believe you and then kill us so you can completely shatter my heart a second time?"

It had taken weeks for me to function after everything that had happened to Kaus. Zach had to drag me around to keep me safe during that time, and I owed him my life. I wasn't going to let this bastard kill him or destroy me.

Cor ran his fingers through his hair and then rubbed his face. He slowly shook his head, trying to find the right words.

"Start from the beginning, Cor. Give me all the information you have or so help me, I'll go collect the bounty on your boyfriend's head."

He let out a breath as he took a seat across from me. "Fine. I'll explain." He bit at the dead skin on his lip for a second, then let out another breath. "So I've been trying to get closer to the Silurian to enact my revenge, correct?"

I nodded. "Right. The revenge you haven't gone into detail about."

"I'm sorry... It's just so... I don't know, complicated? I just... I wanted to kill him right away, but that wouldn't be enough—at least not for me. I needed to get close to him, find his weakness and all the things he cherished most. In order to do that, however, I had to get money. The only way to do that, however, was to become a bounty hunter. Well, besides the prostitution, which does bring in some good money, by the way." He gave me a smug look. Leave it to Cor to stop being serious for a moment.

I shook my head. "I did not need to know that."

"Oh, but you did. Anyway, I've been taking on bounty-hunting jobs. Like what you and Zach do."

I wanted to make a comment on how we didn't take jobs from the person who killed our people, but I bit my tongue.

"And yesterday... What did you two do to piss off all the Silurians?"

I shrugged. "Besides existing? I have no idea. A week ago there was... an altercation, but Zach and I only used tranks. Bullets are expensive, and unless people are trying to kill us, we don't use real bullets. I have no idea who killed those Silurians, but they were alive when we left."

Cor sighed. "Well, if you haven't noticed, they want you dead and have hired me to kill you. I thought I could find you two, explain everything, make you go into hiding, and fake your deaths. But now here you are, showing your face to the people who hired me."

That at least made some sense. At least he was trying to do all this without killing us. But nevertheless, here we were—me forcing him to tell me the truth, if it was in fact the truth. He could be making this shit up. The irony if he wasn't, however, was that if we'd waited just a bit longer, he would have had to come to us.

I pressed further. "So that was what the meeting was about? How they wanted you to kill us before we leave?"

"Exactly. On top of all the people who want Gabe dead, we literally can't sleep without one eye open. Especially since both Gabe and Zach are downstairs drinking and being loud."

I let out a laugh as I shook my head. "Sounds about right. Speaking of which, I'm getting hungry. Is there still a buffet?"

He nodded. "There is. But that doesn't solve how we are all going to make it out alive."

I bit my lip. "Well, we could first get something to eat, and then we can plan Krax's murder. Problem solved if we kill the top." I beamed.

He pinched the bridge of the nose. I swore I saw a bruise forming. "There is no way we can kill him without dying in the process."

I stood up. "Don't worry. You have me here. I haven't died yet, and I don't plan to now. You just have to promise me, Cor, you have told me everything. And I mean *everything*."

He hesitated, which totally meant he was lying.

Although he liked to weave truths and lies, I knew when he was lying. "Yeah, you know everything you need to know."

So there was more. I would have to deal with it later or else I would murder him out of pure hunger, as my stomach was now making my emotional decisions for me. "Well then, my dear Cor, let's see what the other two are up to."

CHAPTER XXXI

<u>**Zach**</u>

I was slowly coming down from the buzz. Slowly.

I just couldn't say no to mimosas, and once I had one, I had to have another. That's just how it was with mimosas. As I set my fork down, my stomach now beyond full, I knew Ellie was going to kill me. I was supposed to be watching Gabe, keeping an eye out for anything suspicious, and, well, I didn't fail since he was still sitting next to me, finishing his own plate. I just hadn't stayed alert like I needed to.

And there was the whole thing with Byron. Would I have noticed him earlier if I hadn't had a drink? Or would he have snuck up on us as quickly? There was no way to be certain, and honestly, I doubted there would have been a way for us to stay here without him noticing, which brought up another matter.

I glanced at the Silurians in the room. They didn't seem to notice us as much as I thought they would, but Silurians were always the hardest to read. They always looked angry with their narrow eyes and slithering tongue. I hated them. They didn't give a care for any other life except their own and thought they were the superior species. How I would love to see them disappear.

They were the reason my people were dead—they were the reason I had no home to go to.

These thoughts always intruded into my mind when I had a couple of drinks. They made me sick, but I couldn't do anything about it. It wasn't fair. None of this was fair. Why was my kind hated so much? Why was everyone I grew up with gone?

"I wonder when Cor is going to come back with Ellie. They seem to be taking a while," Gabe commented, bringing me out of my own dark thoughts.

I wondered if he had noticed or if he was just trying to make conversation.

"Probably in the back, making out or something." My eyes went wide, realizing what I had said. "Or… not."

Gabe laughed. "I really don't care if they do or not. Cor and I don't exactly have a closed relationship. It's fine with me if he loves someone else. I just hope he is up-front about it if anything does come up between the two of them."

I wondered if it was because he knew he had no chance in keeping Cor with everything going on or if he really didn't mind having more than one partner. I supposed it was the latter since he tried to sleep with me a couple of nights before.

"What about you? Have anyone you love?" Gabe asked.

I shrugged. "I mean, I love Ellie, but it isn't anything more than close friendship. Cor was like a brother to me back in the day. Never really have had intimate feelings about anyone, don't know if I really want to."

Gabe nodded. "I can respect that. Sexual love isn't for everyone. It's probably overrated, to be honest. Seems like it some days."

"I think that's because you're dating Cor. He makes

everything seem overrated."

He laughed. "That might be true, but he has a heart of gold. Deep down anyway."

I wasn't too sure of that. I thought his heart was black, even back then. And yet Ellie fell for him. And I saw her eyes light up again when Cor helped her get ready. That love was all coming back to her—or perhaps it never left.

The story Cor told us didn't seem far from the truth. He and Ellie were truly in love, and we grew up in such poor conditions that I wouldn't put it past him to take up some stranger's offer to give him an education so he could go to a university. Then he could get an acceptable job to provide for her. It was actually admirable if it were in fact true. I still felt as if I couldn't trust him as I didn't know if all this was a lie and he had something up his sleeve. But if I were honest, he was acting like a man who had nothing to lose—that he just wanted to destroy the thing that took everything away from him.

Ellie and I knew that feeling all too well.

The two of them were a lot alike. Nothing could stop Ellie or Cor when they came up with a plan. If Cor was just more honest with what he intended to do, then perhaps both of them could succeed. But Cor liked to keep secrets as much as Ellie liked to cause trouble. As I said, two peas in a pod.

"Zach, did you really down a bunch of mimosas?" I heard Ellie's voice behind me. Crap, I was in trouble.

I turned to find her hand on her hip. Standing next to her was Cor. "I see you found each other."

"Yeah, we did," she commented, but didn't go into it any further. I had a feeling there was more to that statement. "And he told me that you were drinking on the job."

I pointed at Gabe. "He offered, and I couldn't refuse. I figured with how much food I was eating, it would be fine."

Ellie rolled her eyes. "Whatever. I'm starving. Let's get some food, Cor."

He nodded. "Yeah, I'm starving."

I watched as he placed his hand on the small of her back and guided her to the buffet. Yeah, by the time this was all over, they would be together again. I shook my head in disagreement. She had been ready to kill him, and yet there she was, falling for that cute face all over again.

But perhaps that was what both of them needed—to

find each other.

Or perhaps Ellie was letting her heart do the talking since she couldn't deal with all the other emotions swirling inside. She didn't like to show what was on her mind, and sometimes I wondered if she would ever be able to love again. This was either going to end horribly or it would be a happily ever after. More than likely, it would be the former.

The two of them came back with large plates covered with everything that was offered. It always amazed me how well Ellie could fill a plate without mixing any of the food. It almost made me hungry again. Almost.

I leaned over and whispered into Ellie's ear. "Lord Byron visited. Pretty much warned us he was going to try to murder Gabe again, all bad-guy-like."

She let out a sigh. "And we have a bounty on our heads from the Silurians up here. Cor was given instruction to kill us."

My eyes widened. And she still had a thing for this man? "Well, great. We are going to have a great time. Poker tournament starts tomorrow, right? Then the whole ceremony to get Gabe inducted is a week, and then we are free to leave."

"Right. So we just have to survive that long." She

made it sound easy. Typical.

"Sweet. Easy as pie."

"Just don't drink too much."

I stuck out my tongue. "Fine. I'll just go practice my poker for tomorrow."

"Have fun. You need all the practice you can get."

I stuck my tongue out at her again and headed over to the tables. As Cor had mentioned before, there were many tables in here. We would have to make our way upstairs to the poker level to really see how people played, but this would be a good start. I found a table that wasn't too busy—only had a Lyran female and Sirian male. I sat the farthest from both of them, and they didn't pay me much mind. I gave the dealer my room number, and he gave me a stack of chips.

Poker wasn't my favorite game, but I was quite decent. Although it did take skill, it also took luck, which honestly I didn't feel I had when looking back on my life. Or perhaps I did have it, and that was why I had survived so long. I just didn't have the right kind of luck. Yeah, that felt accurate.

An hour passed, and Ellie, Cor, and Gabe were still chatting away at their table. A couple more people joined my table, and it was now full. I figured once a chair opened up, they would come over, or perhaps they would come once they wanted to go upstairs. Or perhaps they were waiting for me to lose all my money and come back to them crying.

Well, that wasn't going to be far off here soon. My stacks were slowly dwindling. Perhaps Ellie was right —I did suck.

The human that had taken a seat next to me cashed out and got up to leave. I glanced over to Ellie to see if they were going to head over to take his place. Before they could do anything, however, a different figure sat down next to me.

It was Byron.

My entire body froze as the dealer gave him a stack of chips and dealt him in. My eyes moved to Ellie, who saw what had just happened. She began to stand when I slowly shook my head.

"Well, well, it seems we meet again, Zachariah."

I turned and gave him a large smile. "It seems we have. Such a small gambling hall on this moon, don't you think?"

He glanced around. "You're right. I've seen larger, though much of the action is upstairs. But I'm glad I got to come and chat with you again. There are some things

I want to discuss. But it's rather crowded here. Would you mind coming back to my room with me?"

I felt something jab into my side. Peering down, I was not surprised to find his revolver bruising my rib cage. I didn't let the fake smile escape my lips.

"Of course. Wouldn't have it any other way."

Byron turned to the dealer. "If you will excuse us, we have some business to take care of."

I glanced at Ellie one more time. She had seen it all, so at least she would know where I was and what had happened. I just hoped that she wouldn't do anything stupid and cause us all to be killed.

CHAPTER XXXII

<u>Cor</u>

Well, this all got more complicated really fast.

I held Ellie down by her shoulders before she could do anything stupid. Whatever that man was doing wasn't good. Nothing good came of that man.

"Let me go," she growled.

"We can't make a move against him—if we do, he will kill Zach right then and there. Or worse, he will reveal who both of you are and there will be a moon full of Silurians after you."

She pursed her lips but stopped resisting me.

"He is my best friend, Cor. If anything happens, I don't know what I will do."

"Zach can take care of himself. I doubt he will hurt him. Now, do you want to explain to me how you know that man and why he would go after Zach?"

Ellie frowned. "That is Lord Byron. He was the one who hired us to kill Gabe in exchange for information on your whereabouts."

I frowned. That was not good. "He's the one who hired you?"

Ellie nodded. "Yup. And it seems even though we gave the money back, he didn't like that we didn't finish our mission. I suppose he'll give us a ransom later. He won't kill Zach, at least. Probably. Hopefully. I mean, Zach can take care of himself. He's made it this far... and if he wants me to finish the job, he won't kill him."

I glanced to where the man named Byron took Zach, wondering if I should tell Ellie the truth of who that man was. If I did, however, she would go straight into action and risk everything. No, I had to keep this a secret. It was for the greater good.

"I think he'll be fine," I said. "You are right. There

will be a ransom first."

"Lord Byron has been in the society for quite some time," Gabe added. "He doesn't like when new people like me try to join. He will keep Zach alive, although once he gets what he wants, he might kill both of you, and Cor for good measure."

Perhaps Byron also liked to lure young teens into thinking he cared for them and destroy everything they had. I let out a breath slowly. I needed to focus. I needed to finish this mission. No matter the cost. This was only a hiccup. I would take care of it.

I stood up. "I'm going to go get us tickets for tomorrow. Do you think I should grab one for Zach?"

Ellie shook her head. "No, I think he'll still be Byron's collateral. Besides, he sucks at poker and probably lost you some money already."

I let out a breathy laugh. "Great. Well, I'll get that underway. Keep an eye on Gabe. And Gabe, don't let her do anything foolish."

She eyed me as she also stood up. I could see her arms were still shaking. I wanted to help her get Zach back, but at this point, we had to just let it all play out. "Shall we go practice some poker, Gabe?"

He stood up and held out his arm. "Yes, we shall."

I was glad to see that they were getting along, but that didn't mean we were out of the frying pan. Or perhaps we were, and we had already gone straight into the fire.

No, I had a feeling the fire would be worse. Much worse. And not only that, but the fire would be when we got the ransom note. Because nothing ever went according to plan. Ever.

I tried to rub the migraine that was beginning to form out of my head as I made my way to the front desk. A familiar Sirian manned the desk. She smiled, her sharp, almost sharklike teeth as white as snow.

"Well, if it isn't Cornelius. What can I do for you today?"

I leaned forward and gave the woman I had slept with the night before a grin. "I would like to get three tickets for tomorrow's poker tournament."

She raised an eyebrow, but I saw the faint blush on her cheeks. "You know as well as I that each player has to register themselves."

I glanced at her name tag. Right, her name was Jubilee. I gave her another smile. "Come on, Jubilee, for me? You know we can pay for it. I just need three places in the tournament."

"It would be one thing if you were just buying for Gabriel, but who is the other person? Have they been background checked?"

As if these rich people had clean backgrounds. I grabbed her hand and kissed it. "You think I would vouch for anyone indecent? You know I have a good eye for people." I gave her a little wink.

Her cheeks blushed even more, causing her to fluster. "Cornelius, I don't want to risk my job…"

"You won't. I promise. And perhaps you could persuade me to stop by tonight as well…"

She bit her lip, which to me looked like it hurt. I mean, I would know—some of these Sirians were biters. "Fine. But if I get caught, you're in deep trouble."

I leaned over the desk and gave her a kiss on the lips. "Thank you so much."

She typed a few things in her computer and handed me three badges with lanyards. "Good luck tomorrow. And don't forget, my room number is B2. I get off just past midnight."

I grinned. "I wouldn't forget."

I turned back and headed to find Ellie and Gabe. One thing down, a few more things to go.

I didn't know where to start for the rest. Did I figure out how I was going to make it look like I assassinated Zach and Ellie first, or did I go deal with the Zach situation? Zach was more than likely safe for the time being, but I wasn't sure what card that man, who now went by Byron, apparently, was going to pull. It had been years since I had seen him, and I had no idea that he had been the same person after Gabe all this time—I had no idea that Obi was Byron. Or Byron was Obi. I wasn't sure which name was the fake one at this point.

As anyone who lived in the desert knew, when it rained, it poured.

Working out what was going on with Zach and Byron would probably be the best thing to do first.

I had to act like nothing was up to Ellie, though, which wouldn't be easy. She already didn't trust me after finding that folder. I didn't blame her after what had happened. I would do the same if I were in her shoes.

I found her and Gabe working the poker table. She was flirting with the three other men at the table, who were all human. I wondered if they were the same humans who were in league with Byron or if they just happened to be here.

I stepped up to the table. "I see you two are having fun."

Ellie smiled at me. "Yes, we are. I was telling these lovely gentlemen about my home back in the Human Zone and my love for my pet horses." She placed her hand on her heart. "They are like family to me. I would die if anything happened to them while I was away."

So she was as good as me at lying. That was interesting to see. Then again, I felt there were some truths to those statements.

I gave the two of them their badges for tomorrow. "These are for you. Don't lose them as I don't think I'll be able to get any more. Meanwhile, I've some... other business to tend to. I'll meet you at dinner."

Ellie pouted playfully, but I could tell that she was furious I was leaving again as she wanted to know what I was doing. "Oh, so soon. You must play a game with us. I want to wipe the floors with you like I am with these poor men."

I glanced at them. They seemed amused and offended at the same time. Good for her. "Later, I promise. But first, business."

I kissed her hand and then kissed Gabe on the cheek and left for Byron's room. The moment I turned away from them, I felt my face grow cold.

It had been three years, but I would never forget that face. The face that smiled at me and told me how I would make a difference and change how the world viewed Kausians forever. I supposed he wasn't lying in that regard.

I knew where his room was because, well, I always tried to keep all the rooms of those in the society memorized. The thing was, even though we had been up and down from here a few times in the past couple of months, I never had seen him. I just figured he was some other human I didn't have to worry about too much. Clearly I was wrong—clearly he was an even bigger thorn in my side than earlier.

Byron's room was on the same floor as ours but was all the way on the other side of the hotel. I weaved through the hallways and finally found the door. I took a few breaths, calming myself down as my heart was racing—in fear of what this man was up to, especially after all this time.

I knocked on the door, and in a matter of seconds, it opened. Byron smiled as he leaned against the doorway. "Cornelius. Long time, no see. I suspected you would show sooner or later."

"Well, yeah. You showed up out of nowhere, Obi. Or I guess your real name is Byron."

"Lord Byron actually. I have been watching you this entire time but making sure you didn't see me."

"That does explain a lot. I thought perhaps you crawled back into the hole from which you came."

He laughed, although I didn't think my comment amused him that much. "So have you come to save your friend?"

I narrowed my eyes. "What do you want? Why are you doing this?"

He gestured around. "Isn't it obvious? Because I can."

"You know what I mean. Why have you sent assassins after Gabriel? Including Zach and Ellie?"

He raised an eyebrow. "Oh, so you do know them. You know, their payment wasn't just some money. I told them I would give information on your whereabouts. I knew where they would run off to since, well, it was obviously here. I never imagined that Gabriel would reveal he knew you as well. I mean, it was possible. I just had really hoped they would be quick about killing him."

"But why? What do you have to lose with Gabe in

this society?"

Byron slammed his fist on the doorframe. "What do I have to lose? Humans are already a joke, Cornelius. We are seen as being the lowest of the low now that Kaus is gone. You think I'm going to stand by and let Gabriel make a fool of us even more? The other races don't see us as strong or intelligent, but I beg to differ. But I can't change their mind when I have that idiot in the society, now can I?"

There were so many things wrong with that. Sure, Gabe wasn't the brightest of the bunch, but that didn't mean he was an idiot. "I know Gabe is odd, but what makes him different from most humans here?"

Byron's eyes narrowed for a moment, and then he started laughing. "Don't tell me... Do you not know what he is? That is too much. I didn't think he was one to keep secrets."

I shook my head. "I don't understand what you're talking about."

He leaned closer to me, and I was able to get a better look in his room. Tied to a chair was Zach. He didn't appear scared so much as bored. His eyes met mine, and his eyebrow went up. I had a feeling he would try to ask what I was doing there if it weren't for the fact that his mouth was taped shut.

"Your boy Gabriel—he's half Sirian. And because of that, he needs to be killed. Humans are joked about constantly. They laugh at the fact humans with sleep with anything that moves, and all those half-breeds make it worse."

I couldn't believe what I was hearing. Gabe was half Sirian? Why didn't he tell me? It's not like I would care, but that meant he was keeping secrets from me. It wasn't like I could talk, however, as he didn't know I was the reason my zone was destroyed.

But it was still a crush to my heart.

"So what? Are you going to try to kill all half-breeds on the planet?"

He grinned. "Perhaps. Now, I have a little on my plate right now between threatening your friend and sending a ransom note to your other friend. Perhaps we can chat later."

With that, he closed the door in my face. I thought about kicking it down and saving Zach right then and there, but by the sounds of it, he was going to keep him alive. I just had to make sure Gabe survived all this. I pounded my fist on the door.

Why did this all have to spiral out of control?

CHAPTER XXXIII

<u>Ellie</u>

Was Cor not staying around because he knew that I would go after Zach if he were watching Gabe, or did he really have other business to attend to? And if so, what business could he be doing? I supposed it could be prostitution, but if that were the case, I had a feeling he would be up-front about it.

Theses thought swarmed my mind as the poker game kept going. That didn't matter—these men did not know how to play well. At first they convinced themselves they were losing to make a girl feel good, but we were all far beyond that, and they knew it. I noted how they each shifted in their chairs and stopped smiling as I had won hand after hand.

The tournament should be easy.

The dealer flipped over the last card. It was a queen of hearts, which was perfect since a jack of hearts and ten of hearts had already been played and I had a king and ace of hearts in my hand.

The first man bet the rest of his chips. Poor sap—he was going to lose it all. The other two matched his best, more than likely thinking I couldn't possibly have a royal flush.

I, of course, met their bet. Gabe had folded already, so now it was time to reveal our cards.

"Well, dear sirs, I do believe you have lost another round. What do you say? Should I buy a round of drinks to make up for your loss?" I turned to a waiter. "A round for all these gentlemen, on me."

"You better be careful, lass," a man with graying black hair commented. "You might use all your luck today and lose the tournament tomorrow."

I grinned. "You all would love that, wouldn't you? But Lady Luck has always been on my side, and I don't see tomorrow being any different." At least in gambling. In life, however, that was a completely different story.

"Maybe I should just forfeit tomorrow then, save myself the pain."

I placed my hand on his shoulder playfully and pouted. "Where would the fun be in that? Please tell me you will come tomorrow."

The man smiled a cocky smile. "Well, for you, perhaps I will."

Gabe gave me a look that I knew meant something along the lines of *so it's not just Cor who can flirt with anything that moves.* I ignored it and stood. "Well, I think I'm going to pull out of this game before the rest of you lose your money. It has been a pleasure. Gabe, shall we go find our friend and have some dinner?"

He nodded as he stood. "Yes, that sounds like a good idea."

We made our way to the elevator. Cor had mentioned that the restaurant was on the top of the hotel. It would be a lie to say I wasn't excited to see what the roof was like at this place. I imagined it was spectacular. With everything going on, I hadn't been able to appreciate the views I knew I would never get to see again.

Except I felt guilty if I enjoyed them now without Zach.

He was more than likely fine, as Byron would just want collateral. But that didn't mean the human wasn't torturing him or something. I bit at my nails as we stepped inside the elevator. If he was suffering, it would be my fault.

"We should probably change," Gabriel commented before he pressed a button. "As in, we are going to go change into our fancier outfits whether you like it or not."

"Fine," I said even though I didn't want to. I hated the dress I was already in and had a feeling I would hate the next one just as much.

The elevator went to our floor. Since Byron was human, he was more than likely holding Zach in one of these rooms. I glanced around but saw no sign of either of them. There were many rooms on this floor, and it would be inconvenient if I kicked all of them down.

Gabe scanned his key card, and as we opened the door, we found Cor sitting on the couch with his head in his hands. When he heard the sound of the door, he flinched and grabbed his gun. His face softened as he realized it was us.

"Oh, you scared me."

"Have you been here the entire time?" I asked. "Wallowing in self-induced misery?"

He shook his head. "No. Had a couple of things to discuss with people. Was wrapping my head around it all before I went and found you."

I placed my hand on my hip and raised an eyebrow. "The webs we weave, eh? You going to talk about it now, or are you going to wait until it all explodes in your face?"

He rubbed his face again. "I'm going to go with the latter for now."

I rolled my eyes as I went toward my room. "Still no word of Zach?"

"Nope. I have a feeling Byron is keeping him and we will be getting a ransom soon."

I didn't like that one bit. Zach was like a brother to me—my best friend through thick and thin. I kept telling myself that he was fine—we didn't die easy—but that didn't mean I couldn't worry. It was eating at my stomach, and I wanted to throw up, but I somehow was also hungry. I just didn't know what to do.

The problem was that if I tried to go save him, we wouldn't be able to get off this moon alive—not with how many Silurians there were. At least with Zach with Byron, I didn't have to worry about a Silurian finding him. The Silurians would be looking for both of us, and now that we were separate, we wouldn't stand out as much. At least there was that.

"I guess I will go change. Gabe said we were supposed to wear fancier clothes?"

Cor let out a breath. "Yeah, a fancier dress would be good."

I went into my room and opened the closet door. I stared at the dresses, and the dresses stared back at me, knowing I was an impostor. I turned my head to shout into the other room. "Cor… I need help…"

I heard him audibly sigh as he got up to help me pick something out. He entered my bedroom. "Do you really need my help to pick out a simple dress? Aren't you used to seducing guys and whatnot?"

"Yeah, nothing this fancy. I'm used to going to bars and shindigs that don't necessarily deal with money of this magnitude."

He let out a breath. "Fair enough. Let me help pick something out."

Cor flipped through the dresses that were hung up. He pulled out a red dress that showed a little more skin than I thought was proper. It was both frilly and revealing.

"You can't be serious."

"Oh, but I can. Luckily your hair is still holding up quite nicely, so all we need to do is change your makeup a bit."

"Yippee…," I commented.

Cor stepped forward and began to try to unbutton my top.

I jumped back. "What in the goddess's name do you think you're doing?"

"Helping you get undressed. I saw you in your underwear this morning. I didn't think you cared."

"Seeing me in underwear is different from physically undressing me."

"Sorry, it's just habit."

I rolled my eyes. "Right, all your whoring."

He grinned. "What, are you jealous?"

"As if." I unbuttoned my top and stepped out of my skirt. I grabbed the red dress and found the buttons to undo before slipping it over my head. Cor carefully helped me not tangle my hair and buttoned it up in the back. I had to admit he was good at this sort of thing.

"Also," Cor began, "I'll have a job tonight. Around

midnight, if you catch my drift."

"What, was that how you got our badges for tonight?"

"Naturally."

It shouldn't matter to me what he was up to, but I felt the strange ping of jealousy in my chest. What was wrong with me? He was taken, and he was sleeping around for money or things he needed. That was not relationship material—at least not the type of relationship I was going for.

But he would be open to it. He and Gabe clearly had an open relationship, so there would be no harm in asking. I pushed back all the thoughts. I had spent three years hating this man. Could I really fall for him all over like this? Was the pain I was feeling all these years not hatred but heartache? And now that I knew the truth —that he had been doing all those secret things for a better life with me—could I fall in love with him all over again?

"You all right?" Cor questioned.

I blinked and nodded. "Yeah. Let's get this makeup thing over with."

Cor finished up my makeup, and I hardly even

recognized myself. I looked like one of those harlots one would see on the covers of books or magazines. I was glad no one we knew would see me like that.

As Cor and Gabe finished getting ready, I heard something slide under the door. I grabbed a knife from the kitchen as I quickly and quietly peered into the hallway. There was no one there. I reached down and picked up the paper. The outside had my name written on it.

It was from Byron.

I went to my room and closed the door. Quickly, I unwrapped it and found the ransom note.

IF YOU WANT YOUR FELLOW KAUSIAN TO REMAIN ALIVE, YOU MUST MAKE GABRIEL SIT AT THE TABLE CLOSEST TO THE DOORWAY TOMORROW AND LEAVE HIM THERE.

I stared at the letter. That was the most random order I had ever read. Was this even a ransom? I had to make him sit there? What in the gods' names did that mean?

There was only one way to find out.

CHAPTER XXXIV

<u>Zach</u>

Well, I had been in worse prisons. And worse hotel rooms. And held captive by worse people. All in all, this was probably my most pleasant experience being kidnapped.

I wasn't sure if that was a good thing, but at least I was comfortable. Someone knocked at the door, and one of the human guards who were watching me opened the door. A human waiter with dark hair wheeled the tray in. He didn't even care that I was tied to a chair at the table and had tape over my mouth. Perhaps he was used to it; perhaps it was because he noticed I was Kausian as my eyes were no longer covered with glasses. Either way, he placed two plates on the table, took the covers off, and left the room, not asking any questions.

The guard ripped the tape off my face, which took some of my beard hair with it.

"Ow…" I pressed my lips together as I couldn't rub the injury with my bound hands.

"Eat," the guard motioned to the food.

I stared down at it, trying my best not to drool. I took in the sweet scent of ham, grilled vegetables, mashed potatoes, cobbler, cheesy noodles, and some things I couldn't identify. "How am I supposed to eat if my hands are still tied?"

"I will unbind you if you promise not to try anything funny. If you do, then you won't be eating again for the rest of your time here."

"I promise not to try anything, especially with that warning."

The large man let out a laugh. "I thought so. I saw you chow down at the buffet today. You seemed like a man who likes his food."

"That I do. And my exercise. Perhaps I can take a walk around…"

"I'm not that stupid. But I'll untie one arm to eat with."

He untied my right hand, and I grabbed the fork and began to stuff my face. I had no shame—I was starving. Besides, I didn't know if they would be so generous as to feed me again.

We ate in silence as I didn't know what to say to this guy nor how much he knew. I thought about earlier that day when I heard Cor at the door. He called Byron a different name—he called him Obi. Was Byron the man who had tricked him all those years ago? If so, then was Byron one of the men who had led to the destruction of my home?

Before I could ask him anything, Byron left me alone with whatever guard was around. So far, I'd had three different guards—all human. I noticed a theme going on—a theme of Byron only liking humans. It was no wonder he had it out for Gabe as he was clearly racist and an asshole, but with Gabriel, it seemed a bit more personal. He could have just made sure he wasn't welcomed into the society. No, he wanted him dead for a different reason, but I wasn't sure why exactly that was.

I shifted in my chair. My ass was getting sore sitting for hours, and I had a feeling that they weren't going to give me a bed for the night. At least they weren't torturing me. Not yet anyway.

I finished up the meal, as did my guard, and he tied my right arm back down. So far, it didn't seem I had much to worry about, but I also hadn't talked to Byron about what his plan was and what he was going to do with me. He was there for a while until Cor showed up, and then he left to take care of business. I had no idea when he would be back.

Now that I was full and could think straight, I tried to figure out how I would get out of there. It didn't seem Byron wanted me dead. He was just using me as a hostage to get Ellie to do his bidding. If he was indeed the Obi that Cor spoke of, then he knew more about our situation than we'd originally realized—not to mention he didn't care for Kausians. Perhaps after this was over, he would kill us all.

At least we had some time to figure it out. If he really wanted us dead, I had a feeling we would be dead. He could have simply pointed out to the Silurians we were here, and we would probably be dead by now or at least out of his hair. He was planning something, and I needed to figure out what it was.

As if the bastard knew I was thinking of him, the door of the room opened, and Byron stepped in. I felt my body freeze. He seemed different from when we first met. Back then, he seemed like any other elite—snobbish and willing to use money to get what he wanted. Now he appeared like a villain in a play. He was good at holding himself how he wanted people to perceive him—I would give him that. All he needed now was a mustache he could twirl.

"Leave us," he said to the guard. The guard nodded and left the room.

I gulped. "So has Ellie killed all your men yet?"

He chuckled. "No, she has not. I gave them my word I will keep you safe if they do what I say. She has been given a note, and I assume she will perform the task nicely. Your girlfriend doesn't have any real ties to Gabriel, and I presume she will trade his life for yours."

"She's not my girlfriend," I interjected, as if it mattered. "We are just best friends."

"Right, she was the one for whom Cornelius was working so hard for. He wanted to give her a normal life. That's even better. She'll help me kill Gabriel so that he is out of her way of getting Cornelius back."

I shook my head. "Nah, she wouldn't do that. She's not selfish. Besides, I'm not quite sure she likes him anymore after what happened."

Byron's lips turned up in a crooked smile. "Is that so? Well, I would disagree, but that is just me. I think she'll do as I ask, and with that I can move on to the next part of my plan."

"Which is what exactly? So far I haven't been able to figure it out."

"To rid the world of filth, of course."

I frowned. "That doesn't make sense. What filth?"

He laughed. "It's hard for you to see because you're part of the filth. You're a half-Kausian. And as long as there are other species that humans can intermingle with, then there will always be filth."

I tried to put the pieces together in my head, but the more I thought about it, the more disgusted I was. "So you're saying you want to destroy all half humans and all other races because they aren't full human?"

"Precisely."

"That's crazy, not to mention impossible. And just"— I shook my head, disgusted with what I was hearing— "wrong. There isn't anything bad or filthy about people loving each other and having a family. It's assholes like you who make it hard to live in this world."

"Because you shouldn't be here—none of the other races should be here. They bring chaos and problems. If only humans were to take over this planet, then there would be no more war or anything holding us back. We wouldn't be seen as an inferior race."

"That makes no sense. Humans won't be able to run this planet any better than any other races. Besides, the other races would just unify. It's impossible."

"Is it? I just have to get all the nations to turn on each other, just like I did for the Kausians."

My eyes narrowed. "That was the Silurians. They are the ones who hated us and led that attack."

He laughed. "You think they always hated you? Do you think your kind has always been hated by everyone? Far from it. Your kind used to be worshipped until two generations ago. Until my grandfather began his plan that he passed down to me."

I didn't know how to respond—I didn't know if I should call his bluff or if I should keep quiet to see if he would go on. Either way, the food I had eaten earlier was threatening to come back up to visit.

Byron went on, more than likely noticing my sick,

unbelieving eyes. "My grandfather planted the seeds of distrust against your kind, or half your kind. Slowly, people thought Kausians were up to no good, and by the time my father was in the society, almost everyone hated the Kausians. I was the one who was able to get the final push to destroy your kind. And tomorrow I'll be the one to give the final push to destroy the Silurians. Or at least make it so that no one will trust them every again."

It took a second for this information to register. It was because of him and his family that my life had been destroyed—that everything was destroyed. And now he was going to do it all over again with the Silurians.

"Why?"

He laughed. "I already told you—because I want the humans to survive. We need to survive, and in order to survive, we must destroy any who might turn on us. We must go on the offensive instead of waiting for someone else to attack."

"That's crazy-person talk! All our kind used to live in harmony, and it was because of you that we aren't anymore!"

Byron slapped me across the face. "I am not crazy! I

am bringing order!" He took a deep breath. "Consider yourself lucky. I need you for the next part of my plan. And then I will kill you, of course."

I couldn't believe what I was hearing. This person was a lunatic. I was stuck in this room with a madman.

I just prayed I would get out of this alive and that Ellie knew what she was getting herself into.

CHAPTER XXXV

<u>Gabe</u>

I felt horrible.

It was my fault Zach had been captured. I prayed to the goddess that Byron wasn't hurting him. Zach was not only half human but also a Kausian. Byron was the worst kind of scum out there—one that believed in purity, whatever that meant.

"So what do you think we should do?" Ellie asked as she held up the ransom note.

Byron wanted me to sit at the edge of a room—more

than likely so he could murder me. I turned to Cor. "What do you think?"

Cor rubbed his shaven face. "I think I have had more migraines in the past few hours than I have had in my entire life." He took a seat on the couch and sighed. "We need to come up with a plan, but I can't think of anything that would be good enough."

"Don't we have a bulletproof vest you got a while back?"

"You mean the one you complained was heavy and itchy and swore you would never wear because you didn't think someone would actually shoot you?"

I nodded. "Yeah, that one."

He sighed. "That will help a little. But you are still risking him shooting you in the head."

I shrugged. "I'm done running away from him. We will end this here and now."

"With your possible death."

Ellie folded her arms in front of her chest. "We have to do something to save Zach though. Do you have any other ideas?"

Cor shook his head. "No. I don't."

"Well then," she said. "Either we have to play this out, or we can figure out what room he is staying in and kick the door down and save Zach."

"That will get Zach killed," Cor answered. "And probably us as well."

"Then what should we do?"

Cor bit at the dead skin of his lip. He was always quick to come up with ideas, but this time even he was perplexed. That meant only one thing—there was no other way out of this.

"Let's do what he says," I finally commented. "I don't want to risk Zach's life for mine. This is my mess —not his."

Ellie shook her head. "Zach and I were the ones who took the job. It isn't your fault."

"But you saved me—you could have killed me and collected your bounty. But you didn't. So this is my turn to help you both. I will do whatever it takes."

Cor slapped his hands on his legs. "Fine. We will do it. You will wear the vest, and we will keep an eye out for him during the tournament. But if anything happens, Gabe"—he shook his head—"I will never forgive you."

I gave him a half-hearted smile. "Well, that won't matter since I will be dead."

Before Cor could counter with a witty comment, Ellie's stomach growled so loud it echoed through the room. Both Cor and I stared at her.

"I think my stomach gave up on hurting and went straight to hunger," she said.

Cor stood up. "Well then, I guess we will go up to the restaurant for dinner."

The restaurant on the roof of the casino was just as I remembered it. It was encased in a giant glass dome that revealed the rest of the moon and the planet Maldek below. I loved the view but had grown partially used to it.

Ellie, on the other hand, had not.

She gasped so loud that nearby tables turned to give us an annoyed look. Ellie didn't seem to care as she hurried to the window. At least she wasn't pressing her face against it.

I went to the hostess. "Is it possible to get a table near the window?"

She glanced at her schedule. "I can make that happen." The women glanced at Cor and winked. "Anything for the two of you."

I tipped my hat to her. "Why, thank you. You are most helpful."

The hostess grabbed a couple of menus and led us to

a table. Ellie, after staring out the window for a bit longer, joined us.

"Did you guys see the view?" she asked as she sat down. "It's beautiful."

"I have," Cor smiled. "It's almost as beautiful as it is on the Ferris wheel in the park."

"Right. That was extra special since we sneaked in that time."

"Shh, keep your voice down. They might hear us and come arrest us again," Cor said.

They both laughed, and I was beginning to feel like a third wheel. My chest felt constricted, and I adjusted my tie a little. It didn't help.

"So," I began. "Ferris wheels are fine, but transports make you both sick?"

Cor nodded. "Yup. Almost all Kausians get sick on the space transport, but not as many on trains and amusement park rides. Isn't that right, Ellie?"

"Yeah, I faintly remember Zach getting sick on a rollercoaster or two, but he doesn't get sick on trains."

"Fascinating." I didn't care. I was just hoping to change the mood. It didn't work.

"Remember when we got stuck on that train during the snowstorm?" Cor's eyes were bright, even under his glasses. "That was so bumpy!"

"Not as bumpy as it was when there was that monsoon in Kaus and we were trying to get back before our parents found out we traveled outside the zone."

"Oh yeah! I completely forgot about that. Wasn't that the day your brother moved out?" Cor asked.

The light in Ellie's eyes faded as her lips stopped smiling. "Oh yeah. It was."

The table grew quiet as Ellie scanned over the menu. I had a feeling, since most of Kaus was destroyed, that her brother was among those who passed. Part of me was happy that the two of them were no longer talking about happy memories, as I had felt left out, but I also felt guilty.

Time went by quietly, and more and more guilt rose up. All of us ordered our dinners and waited silently for them to be delivered to our table. After a bit, Cor stood up.

"Excuse me. I need to use the restroom."

He left us sitting there. I had a feeling that was a lie and he didn't want to sit at this table any longer. I reached for my glass of wine, when I accidentally knocked over Ellie's small purse.

It hit the ground and flung open, spilling everything

inside.

"Oh, I'm sorry. Let me help." I bent down to help her grab her stuff.

"It's fine, there isn't much in here."

She was right—all that was in her purse were some knives, a key card that I didn't know Cor gave her, and a familiar-looking ring. I snatched it up and examined it. Sure enough, it was the same as Cor's.

"Where did you get this?" I asked as I handed it back to her.

Her cheeks were bright red. "I… Cor gave it to me. A long time ago. Why?"

"Oh, he has the same one he carries."

"He does? I—" She shook her head. "Don't worry about it. It means nothing now. He's your boyfriend. He has no interest in me."

She says it meant nothing and yet three years later, they both kept carrying it. I had questions—questions I would be bringing up to Cor whether he would like it or not.

The awkward dinner finally ended, and we retired back to the hotel suite. Ellie went straight into her room and closed the door. Neither of them really talked for the rest of the dinner, and I wasn't sure what was worse—being the third wheel or being stuck in the middle of awkward silence for an hour. More than likely, it was the latter.

Cor went into our room and prepped for his job that night. He had told me he was having sex with the reception clerk as payment for the poker entry. I didn't care about that as that situation was normal for us, but it still bothered me he had the ring in his pocket.

He riffled through his suits, looking for the perfect one. I stepped up behind him, fidgeting with my sleeve. This was not the easiest question to ask.

"Hey, Cor?"

"Yeah?"

"Were you ever going to tell me the ring you had in your pocket was a wedding ring?"

He paused for a moment, then turned to me. "Why does it matter? You never cared before."

"Well, since we have been together for two years, I figured the person had passed away and you didn't want to talk about it."

"And how do you know that's not the case still?"

Was he really going to try to lie to me now? "Uh, because it's clear you and Ellie used to be lovers, and she has the exact same one she carries around with her too."

His eyebrows furrowed. "She still has that, right?"

That was not the response I was hoping for. "Yes, it fell out of her purse during dinner."

Then he made an even worse expression—a soft smile.

"Cor, do you still love her?"

He laughed. "What does that matter? You and I have an open relationship—we have sex with other people all the time."

"Yeah, but that is different—that's not about love. I just... I just want to know whether you are going to leave me for her."

Cor shook his head. "That's preposterous. Ellie came up here to kill me. Do you really think she would want to be in a relationship with me?"

"I don't care what she wants—I want to know if you still want a relationship with her. I want to know why you never told me about her. It's clear you knew she was alive all this time, so what was your end game? What are you trying to accomplish? Who have you always seen yourself with?"

He turned back to the wardrobe. "This isn't a

conversation I want to have right now. We have a lot on our plate, Gabe. Let's not make it messier than it has to be."

"I have always let you have your secrets, but I need to know the truth once and for all—do you or do you not still love her?"

Cor faced me and smiled, but it wasn't a happy smile. "My secrets? Well, Gabe, what about your secrets? Why did you never tell me you were half Sirian? And that is why there are men after you? And while Byron never said exactly why he has it out for you, I have a feeling there is some history there. So while we are on the subject of secrets, how about you confess some of your own as well?"

I frowned. When had Byron told him that? "I... I didn't know if you would have accepted me."

"I would have. That doesn't matter to me. And I don't care you have secrets, Gabe. Just don't get on my case about mine if you aren't going to come clean yourself."

I couldn't deny he had a point there. Standing there like an idiot, I was silent. Cor stared at me for a moment longer, then shook his head.

"I figured. Well, I have a job to do, so see you in the morning."

With that, he didn't change but left the suite, not wanting to finish our conversation. I felt bad as he had a point—I had many secrets of my own, and this wasn't the time to bring up everything. But I might die tomorrow, and I didn't want to die not knowing the truth.

Collapsing on the bed, I curled up in a ball and prayed that when I woke up, everything would go back to normal.

CHAPTER XXXVI

<u>Cor</u>

It was going to be fine. Everything was going to be fine.

I knew that wasn't true, but I had to keep telling myself that. I just wanted to take a vacation for a good month, or year even, and not deal with any more assholes. But alas, I had to. Everything was at stake.

After this, I could take out the Silurians and get my revenge on the race who destroyed Kaus. Then I could die in peace. I didn't care what happened to me, to be honest. I just wanted to see the look on Krax's face as he watched his people die a gruesome death.

Getting up out of bed, I found that Gabe was dressed and ready to get the day started. He adjusted his tie in the mirror and noticed me watching him in the reflection.

"You got back late last night."

We hadn't quite finished our talk, which was why I stayed with Jubilee a little longer than I needed to—hoping he would be asleep when I got back. Thankfully, he was. "Yeah, she put me to work since her job was on the line to get Ellie a ticket."

He didn't turn to face me. "I see."

I hated discussing important things, like relationships and all that. It was the reason I liked him so much—normally he was passive and didn't care what I did. But now all of a sudden he was asking me hard questions that I didn't even know the answers to.

"Look, Gabe…"

Gabe shook his head. "Forget about it. We will discuss everything after this is over. In the meantime, you can do whatever you want."

Collapsing back on my pillow, I let out a huff. I didn't know what I wanted. I loved Gabe—he was easy and funny and had the cutest smile, but there hadn't been a day that went by where I didn't think about Ellie. She and I had history—she and I were the same race. It wasn't that I cared about loving someone of a different race, but she knew what it was like being Kausian—she knew how I felt being ridiculed, beaten, and abused. Not to mention she was beautiful, strong, unique, and scary when she was mad.

And I knew the moment I ran that I would regret it for the rest of my life.

I didn't expect to face her again—I didn't expect her to believe my story. No, I expected her to be my end, and I would have deserved it.

But instead, she did listen to my story and was here, looking cute and causing trouble.

Gabe finished what he was doing and went into the main area of the suite. I slowly got up and got ready myself, knowing I more than likely needed to help Ellie put on makeup and do her hair. Jumping in the shower for a quick rinse, I tried to clear my mind and think of what to do next.

Because Byron was going to make his move.

Ellie had been given the letter last night. I was surprised she told us about it instead of hiding it. I knew if I were her, I would have kept it a secret. But now we were able to keep an eye out for whatever strange plan Byron cooked up this time.

More than likely, he was going to shoot Gabe.

If Byron needed him to sit in a certain spot, then it was more than likely there was going to be someone trying to gun him down. Good thing I'd invested in some bulletproof vests. Gabe, I assumed, had already put one on under his suit. He was willing to take the risk whoever shooting him would aim for his chest and not his head. I didn't like having to worry like this—it made me feel like I was having to choose who to help more, Ellie or Gabe.

Which did not make our little fight any better.

I stepped out of the shower and put on a dark suit with a green vest and tie. After making sure it was straight, I headed to Ellie's room, not glancing at Gabe as I knew he was probably eyeing me as I went to help my long-lost love. It didn't have anything to do with me still loving her but the fact that I knew she was standing there not knowing the difference between a neckline from a hemline.

Lo and behold, I was right.

She stood in front of the closet, biting her thumbnail

—something she always did when she was trying to make a decision. It made me smile a little as I missed that look on her face. Her hair was still wet, and her tanned skin contrasted with the white towel that was wrapped around her body. This was not helping me deal with all my buried feelings about her. I quickly closed the door behind me, not wanting Gabe to see that she wasn't properly dressed. Then again, a closed door wouldn't help the situation either.

As if the door closing made her realize someone was in the room, she turned and shot daggers with her golden eyes.

"What did I say about knocking?"

"That it's polite, but I'm not polite, so I didn't see the problem."

She rolled her eyes but didn't kick me out. Did that mean she was more comfortable around me now? Or had she simply given up about her situation—a state of being all too familiar to Kausians?

"I don't know what to wear again. Having options gives me anxiety."

I let out a sigh and walked over to where she was standing. "Let me handle it. Go put some underwear on and dry your hair."

"Fine. Promise not to turn around."

"I'm at least that much of a gentleman."

I peered through the dresses as she put something on and dried her hair. I pulled out a suitable blue dress that was simple enough for a poker tournament. It went to her ankles and wasn't tight, which would give her free range of her legs, and it was sleeveless so she could punch a fellow and not rip anything.

I turned back to her to find her hair frizzy now that she'd dried it. I sighed as I grabbed the brush and tried to fix it. I turned on the curling iron. "You will never change."

"Whatever. I'm just ready for all this to be over."

So she didn't want to stay with me. That made sense —I would want to leave the person who caused this entire mess as well. I should have figured once this was done with, she would be on her way, but it still hurt inside.

"Don't worry, it will be soon. Byron will make his move today, and we can deal with him. Then you and Zach can wash your hands of all this."

She was frowning—her eyes staring in the reflection but not really looking at anything. I knew this look— she was lost in her own mind again.

"Don't worry," I said. "Zach is fine. Byron is just holding him as collateral."

"Do you think our plan will work?"

I nodded. "I do. I think we will make a convincing show for whatever he has planned."

"I hope you're right. Because it should have been me that Byron took—not him. I was the one who agreed to work with him—I was the one who made contact. Zach was just along for the ride."

I didn't know what to say as I knew that feeling all too well. Every night I had dreams of the ghosts of all those who died screaming that it should have been me who was killed, not them.

We remained quiet as I helped her finish getting ready. We had two hours before the tournament would start, and like Ellie, I couldn't wait until it was all said and done.

The poker level was packed with men and women of all races. I watched as Sirians mingled with humans, Lyrans with humans, and Silurians, well, they only mingled with Silurians. I took a deep breath as I noted which tables had Silurians playing cards. Not many of them were good at card games, but they always entered since it was tradition now. Krax was pretty good, but that was more because people didn't like his attitude when he lost and let him win. But this was a tournament, and feelings never got in the way of winning.

The three of us were assigned to different tables. That was both a good and bad thing. It was good as we could cover more area and keep our eyes out for anything suspicious, but it was bad in that now we couldn't easily communicate. We would make do, however, as we always did.

The chips were assigned to each contestant, and the dealer began to shuffle the deck. I took a deep breath and let it out slowly. This would all end fine. Either Byron was bluffing, and nothing would happen, or this would all be over before I knew it. Perhaps one of us would even win the tournament.

Who was I kidding? This was all going to go horribly wrong.

I glanced over at Gabriel, who sat at the edge nearest to the doorway as instructed. He eyed me, and we both turned our gaze to Ellie. She nodded, as if we were having a conversation about how we were going to kick someone's ass or something.

It was Byron's move now.

CHAPTER XXXVII

<u>Ellie</u>

Byron was nowhere to be seen. At least not yet.

The poker tournament had begun, and I watched as all the dealers began laying out the cards—all tented blue, of course, because Cor told me to wear blue glasses today. I hated how much the glasses obscured things, but after so many years of trying to hide my eyes, I got used to it.

As I stayed aware of those who moved near the entrance to the hall, I tried to appear as if this was no big deal for me. I was a rich woman who liked to gamble her money away, just like all the other women in here. Granted, there were only a handful of them, mostly human and a couple of Lyrans and Sirians as well. There were no women Silurians that I had seen. To be honest, I didn't even know what a Silurian woman looked like. Perhaps there were some, and they all appeared like the men—reptilian and covered in leather armor.

The room was obnoxiously loud with people talking on the sidelines, mainly up on the balcony above. I was surprised as all the poker tournaments I had been to were quiet. People laughed and mingled as they took sips of champagne and whiskey as they peered down at us. I wanted whiskey so bad—especially the whiskey I had last night. But I needed to stay alert if I was going to save Zach. I didn't see any sign of his red hair, and the more the clock ticked by, the worse the knot in my stomach became.

He was fine. He had to be fine. Or else…

I didn't want to think about what else. What else meant he was gone, and I didn't know what I would do if Zach wasn't in my life. I would probably murder Byron and anyone close to him in cold blood.

Taking a deep breath, I brought my attention back to the game at hand. The dealer, a Lyran male with gorgeous red-and-white fur, began to deal out our two cards. I picked them up, careful to keep my facial expression the same. It was a king of spades and an ace of diamonds. Those weren't the worst cards by far, but the game was still young.

"Young lady, place your bid," the dealer commented.

I threw in the small blind to get the bidding going, and the next man, another Lyran with gray fur, threw in the big blind. After him was a Sirian woman who appeared to be my age with a gorgeous black dress, and her hair was done up in the most gravity-defying curls I had ever seen. Next were two humans who met the bid. No one added to it, so I placed my other chip down to meet the big blind.

Now that we had everyone's bid, the dealer flipped over the flop. It was a queen of hearts, a king of spades, and an ace of clubs.

Well, those cards were going to make this interesting. If a jack and ten were placed, then we all would have a straight. But if another king or ace was played, I would have a full house.

It was early in the tournament, but I went ahead and

put in a blue chip. I already had a pair with the highest cards in the deck. Odds were, as these people didn't care for money as much as they would at a normal parlor or casino, they would either keep playing because they thought I was bluffing or because they had something higher in their hand. Either way, I would get to learn their habits and tells, which was half of this game.

As I figured, they all met my bid. I noted any gestures they each made and hoped that they would all stay in the game until the end so I could see what their hands were. They were good, I would give them that. The people at this table weren't just playing this tournament for fun—they were professionals. I could see that now.

The next card was flipped. It was a jack of spades.

Well, that definitely made this interesting. I didn't like how I was the first to bid, as I liked to see how others started a round, but it couldn't be helped. I put a red chip in this time.

Although the room itself was loud as the people watching chatted about nonsensical things and drank and ate, all the tables were silent. Everyone was too involved with their hands to make any chit-chat—not to mention any comments might reveal their hands.

One of the humans raised the bid by another red chip. The other human called and so did I. The Lyran next to me also called, but the Sirian folded. Now I knew—if she guided her tongue across her teeth, she more than likely didn't have anything.

I knew that taking the time to learn tells and playing these games would be for nothing since Byron was going to do something soon, but I had to distract my mind—I had to not think about Zach and what would be happening. I kept an eye out, however, for any sign of him or Byron. So far, I didn't see anything.

Peering over at Cor, I found him smiling as he took in all his chips. Of course he was winning—he was great at poker even when we were teens. He was the one who taught me how to read people and how to lie about one's hand and in general. It was no wonder he was so good since he was great at lying as well.

I still didn't know how to sort my feelings out about him. I wanted more than anything to go back to what we had, but I wanted to be back home with our family. And that wasn't possible. I still hated him for lying, but he had lied because he wanted to surprise me—because he wanted to make a life for us. Then all that fell apart in moments.

To be honest, knowing the truth, I couldn't blame him for what the Silurians did. I could, however, blame him for leaving me and Zach when we needed him most —when we needed him to tell us the truth about what happened. I still didn't understand why he ran when we could have teamed up and took down whoever destroyed our home together. Then he went and fell in love with someone else.

Gabe had asked me about the ring he had found in my purse. I didn't know what to say about it but was surprised when he said Cor carried his everywhere he went. I didn't bring it up with Cor this morning as we had a lot more to deal with than our relationship at the moment. But did that mean he still loved me?

But then what about Gabe?

Since our talk last night, Gabe seemed a bit off, but it was hard to say since I didn't know him that well. I know that he talked to Cor last night, and in the Cor fashion, he ran off before the conversation was over. I didn't hear much of the conversation, but it sounded as if they were talking about me.

I blinked my thoughts away. This wasn't the time or place for them. I would have to deal with Cor later.

First, I had to save Zach.

The dealer flipped over the next card. It was an ace of spades.

Full house. Sweet.

"I bid a red chip and two blue chips," I said as I threw my chips into the pot.

The Lyran rubbed his chin. "I'll call." He placed his chips in.

The Sirian had already folded, and the two humans were left. They peered at their cards and at the table. There were a lot of different plays one could have with all the cards that were on the table. There were three spades, so technically someone could have a flush, but my full house still beat that.

"I'll call," the first human said as he grabbed a few more chips. "But I will raise you another blue chip."

Now things were getting interesting. The human beside him tapped his finger on the edge of his card.

"And I will raise another two blue chips," he said as he tossed his own chips in.

I, of course, called that, but I didn't add to the bidding. Next to me, the Lyran furrowed his brows.

"I will fold." He tossed his cards down. Unfortunately, I wouldn't be able to see what he had, but it sounded like he was just trying to call my bluff. I made a note of that in my mind.

The other human called, and we all flipped our card over. One human had two spades, which I figured he would have, and the other had an ace and a queen. I grinned widely.

The dealer nodded to me. "The lady here has won."

I collected my chips. "Thank you, kind sirs, for donating to my cause."

They laughed, but it was for show. Men did not like to lose to women, at least not in my experience.

"Don't get too cocky," one of the humans commented. "The game has only begun."

They had no idea.

An hour passed, and most of the tables were still full, but it was clear who was going to win at each table. Most of the players at my table were losing their money like water in a sieve. But as people were winning and losing, I wondered when exactly Byron was going to attack. So far there was still no sign of him, and if he waited any longer, everyone would be moving and Gabe would no longer be sitting where instructed.

Before I could make my next bid, I heard a gunshot. And another. And another.

But to my surprise, it wasn't Byron or some other humans who were firing their guns, but the Silurians. I took cover and glanced over to Cor, who was as perplexed as I was. What was going on? What were the Silurians doing?

CHAPTER XXXVIII

<u>**Zach**</u>

I stared down from the balcony at the people as they ran to safety. Silurians occupied this floor and were shooting everyone like fish in a barrel. Blood splattered the tables that once were full of chips and cards and fun.

Ellie had taken cover quick enough, which I was thankful for. If this led to her death, I didn't know what I would have done. It would have been all my fault. Cor was fine as well, but he was less of a worry. I didn't

want him dead—not after what he had said—but I also
didn't care about him as much as I did Ellie.

Gabe, on the other hand, was passed out on the floor
with a hole in his back. I felt horrible—his death was on
my hands—his death was because I couldn't say no.

Maybe this was what Cor felt like when he watch
Kaus be destroyed.

"I could not have done this without you." Byron
patted my back. "You were able to transform and
appear just like Krax. All these Silurians believed you
were him. It was perfect. Perhaps I should have kept
Cor around longer—you Kausians come in handy."

I didn't turn to look at him or I might kill him right
then and there. The only thing that was keeping me
from not doing so was the gun in my ribs.

Byron peered down over the edge. "Looks like little
Gabriel has met his demise. It will be much fun to tell
my brother."

I couldn't help asking. "Why would your brother care
about Gabriel?"

"Because, he's his son."

I turned to him. "What? You killed your own
nephew?"

"Indeed, I did. I was betrayed by my own brother,

who had a child with a Sirian. He went against our father's and grandfather's wishes. I couldn't believe it myself when it happened. So I saw to it that he was destroyed. It took a long while—Gabriel may seem weak but is quite hard to kill."

I couldn't believe this man—he had killed his own family due to his racist beliefs. No, this was unacceptable. I had to do something—I had to stop this.

Except that was the second part of the plan.

"Now," Byron said as he jammed the gun into my side. "Turn into a human and help me clean up this filth."

I did as he asked and shifted back to my normal self. "Except you won't give me a gun for some odd reason."

He laughed. "You are a funny one. But no—you are going to stay out of my way and watch." Byron peered down. "Oh look, the guards have finally made it. Let's help them defeat these treacherous Silurians, shall we?"

At least all this death would stop and the people who killed my friends and family would be murdered. But although the Silurians were the ones who physically destroyed my home, it was all because of this man next to me.

Did Cor know that it was Byron who was behind it all? Or did he still think it was Krax?

Byron pulled out another gun and began to shoot the Silurians closest to us. I watched as they fell on the balcony floor or tumbled over the edge and down onto the tables below. I wanted to vomit from all the crimson that stained the entire room and the stench that rose up from below.

Now that there were guards downstairs, the Silurians were getting picked off one by one. They didn't retreat, however, as I, whom they thought was their leader, ordered them to never stand down, no matter the cost. Silurians were loyal, and they would die for their leader.

More and more people evacuated the floor. I peered down and saw that Cor and Ellie were still okay. They themselves had taken down a few Silurians before the guards arrived. I was surprised that more people playing these games didn't carry firearms. Perhaps they thought they were safe since there was no riffraff. They should have known by now that this place was just a tank of sharks.

Byron led me down the stairs to the level that the poker tournament had been held on. The gunfire had ceased as now all the Silurians were dead. Dozens of bodies were scattered across the floor, and I had to look away. Even though it wasn't my first time seeing so much, it still made me sick.

"What happened?" a guard came up to Byron and asked.

Byron shook his head. "It was terrible. The Silurians started attacking. It was a miracle I had my gun with me. I believe I would have been a goner if not."

"The Silurians? Did Krax order this?"

"I most certainly did not!" A voice came from the doorway.

Krax was standing there, bleeding and disheveled. My mouth opened a little in shock as I knew what was supposed to happen—I knew Byron's plan. He ordered his men to detain him and then kill him to bring his body here. It was clear by the wounds on his face that he had escaped.

Byron was equally surprised, which was perfect for me as he was distracted. I leaped away from him and hurried to Ellie, who was still hidden under a table, waiting for all this to play out.

"Thank goodness you are all right!" She wrapped her arms around me.

I squeezed her tight. "I was about to say the same to you."

"What's going on?" She asked as we turned our attention back to the matter at hand.

Byron shook his head. "Everyone saw you, Krax. You ordered your men to kill everyone here. You are trying to do all the other zones what you did to Kaus. You figured if you got rid of the most influential people, it would be easier to take them all down."

Krax shook his head. "No! That is not what happened! This man is a liar!"

Before Krax could go on—before Krax could run straight at Byron and kill him, Byron shot Krax dead.

CHAPTER XXXIX

<u>**Cor**</u>

In an instant, the man I wanted to make suffer—the man whom I had spent the past three year trying to get close to, was dead.

I couldn't believe my eyes.

While I was frustrated—while I wanted to go out there and revive him so I could make him suffer even more by my own hand, I started to put two and two together. This whole time I had believed Krax was behind it all when it was Byron—or Obi when I originally worked with him. At the time, Byron had made it seem like his hands were tied and he had no choice in the matter. After today's charade, however, I had a feeling that wasn't the case.

It was Byron who destroyed my people, not Krax.

But did Byron even have people he loved? Could I make him suffer the same way he had made me suffer? I highly doubted it. So I would have to do something else to make him pay.

I gripped my gun in my hand. I could kill him right then and there and be done with it. As I began to raise my gun, I hand held me back.

"Don't kill him."

I turned to find Gabe had crawled over to where I was still taking cover. I shook my head.

"He tried to murder you, and you want him to live?"

He frowned. "Well, that's complicated. But I don't want you arrested and tried for murder. If we are going to take him down, we have to do it somewhere else."

Gabe had a point there—I would be arrested, if not killed, if I shot Byron. But I didn't know if I would ever have another chance to take my revenge out on him, especially since he knew we found out the truth.

Zach had made it away from Byron and was with

Ellie, so at least we had that going for us. But I doubted Byron was going to let Zach slip away with the information he knew.

Then again, it wasn't as if anyone would believe a couple of Kausians.

"We should try to get out of here before they start questioning everyone. If the clock over there is still correct, there should be a transporter leaving soon," Gabe said. "We can get tickets in the commoners area, buy some clothes to fit in, and be halfway to Mu before Byron notices I'm not dead."

Byron really wanted Gabe dead. Although I knew part of it was due to him being half human, half Sirian, I felt there was more going on. I would have to ask about it later.

"Fine, let's go get Ellie and Zach."

There was still a lot of commotion between the guards coming in and searching for more Silurians, the leader barking orders to sweep the floors, and people looking for friends and family in the pile of bodies that covered the floor. Although it was a terrible, terrible scene, we were lucky we had some cover to get out of there.

We made our way to Ellie and Zach, and Zach's eyes

widened when he saw Gabe.

"You're alive! Thank the goddess. I thought you were dead because of me."

"Well, I mean, you did try to kill me already, so it's not really any different," Gabe replied.

Zach shrugged. "Yeah, well, we didn't, so I still would have felt bad."

"Whatever. We need to get out of here and get on the transport to Mu before Byron can come for us."

Ellie and Zach nodded, and we searched for the best way to get out of there. There were three entrances, with two staircases on opposite sides of the building. As for the elevator, it would be too hectic and busy right about now.

I pointed to the closest door. "If we can get into the hallway, we should be okay. There is a stairwell to the right. Head straight for that."

"Eleven flights of stairs," Zach sighed. "Great."

We crawled through the room toward the hallway, careful to stay out of sight but also away from the dead bodies that littered the floor. There were many, so it was hard. I glanced down at my hands. They were covered in blood. I swallowed back bile as I kept on moving.

Ellie was in front of me and Zach right behind, next

to Gabe. I glanced back to find Byron was still dealing with the guards and Krax's body. He hadn't noticed we were running, but I knew he would soon.

I pushed Ellie to go a bit faster, and she glanced back at me, glaring. "Don't touch my ass."

"Then hurry."

She sighed but did as I asked. We made it into the hallway and stood up. Everyone's knees and hands were covered in blood.

I nodded toward the stairwell. "Let's go."

We started to descend the stairs. I was glad I picked out a dress Ellie could run in as I doubted she would have let me carry her down all this way. Guards started coming up the stairs but didn't pay us any mind since we weren't Silurian.

Honestly, they should have rounded up everyone, but they knew better than to tell rich folk what to do. Byron did a good job convincing everyone that it was just the Silurians that were the culprits. It wasn't as if any other race liked them.

We made it to the main floor. We were almost there —we were going to make out of here alive.

I expected someone to stop us—I expected someone to kill us or shoot us or something. But no one did. In the distance was the spaceship. A bunch of people from the amusement park were gathering to get on the transport.

It was over. We were safe.

CHAPTER XL

<u>**Gabe**</u>

We found a table to sit at, and I went to get drinks as the three Kausians did their best not vomit. I found a place that sold ginger mules and bought four. Hopefully, the ginger would help them get a little better.

Once we got on the ship, we all bought a new change of clothes. Ellie was excited she got to wear pants again even though most women didn't. The suit I got was itchy, didn't quite fit right, but it would do. We didn't want to stand out, after all.

I grabbed the drinks and headed back to the table. Zach was cradling a small trash can I had found earlier, staring down at the ground.

"Here. Ginger mules. They should help."

Taking a seat at the table, I handed everyone their drink. We all sat there for a moment, silent, still processing what happened. Finally, Cor rubbed his face.

"So, Zach, tell us what happened."

Zach held up his finger and hurled into the trash can. He wiped away any filth off his mouth, then downed the ginger mule. Ellie rubbed his back.

Taking a deep breath, Zach answered Cor's question. "Byron is a racist fuck who wants to destroy all other races because they look down on humans, and he thinks they will be their demise. He also really hates half-breeds."

That much I knew. The first time I had met him he said so straight to my face. I took a sip of my drink.

"And since the Silurians are the most powerful currently, he set them up so all the other races would hate them." Cor shook his head. "I can't believe it. I had thought the Silurians were using him three years ago. Never did I imagine that he was the one pulling all the strings."

"I almost did the bidding for the person who destroyed my people." Ellie peered down at her hands. "I'm a monster."

Cor grabbed her hands. "You are not a monster. You had no idea. None of us did."

I stared at Cor's hands as they held Ellie's. I took another sip of my drink, not sure how to feel after all this was over.

Zach nodded to me. "Shall you tell them the whole story of who Byron is or shall I?"

I frowned. So Byron told him about our relationship —another secret I was hiding from Cor. But now Cor knew the truth about what I was, and since all his cards seemed to be on the table, I should go ahead and reveal mine.

The answer came out as a whisper—a squeak, almost. "Byron is my uncle."

Both Cor and Ellie's mouths dropped.

Zach pointed at them. "Hey, that was my reaction too."

Cor was the first to respond to the information. "He's your uncle? And you never thought to tell me?"

My shoulders came up a little, as if I could hide in my own shell. "It never came up."

"I assume you knew he wanted you dead for a while. If you had told me, then I would have been able to keep you safe from him. Gabe, why didn't you say anything?"

I opened my mouth but closed it. I didn't have an answer to that. Because I was ashamed? Because I didn't want him to know my actual troubles? Maybe it was because I thought I would have been too much of a hassle for him and he would have left.

"I don't know. I was just frightened, I guess. I'm sorry. He is my father's brother, but I haven't seen either of them in quite some time. I lived with my mother until I was fifteen and then ran away."

Cor rubbed his temples. "I keep thinking this can't get more complicated, and then bam—another tangle to this web."

"I'm sorry..."

He shook his head. "It's not your fault he's your uncle. You shouldn't be ashamed of who you are, all right? The three of us have had to learn that through the years, so we definitely understand your feeling. Just don't keep any more secrets from me, okay?"

I slowly nodded as Ellie let out a laugh. "You are one to talk, Cor. You always keep secrets. Perhaps it just rubbed off on the poor lad."

Cor shrugged. "What can I say? A man of mystery."

Ellie elbowed him, making Zach laugh. The three of them still got along so well, even after everything that happened. I couldn't say I'd had anyone like that in my life, except for Cor. But now, seeing him like this, I wasn't sure if he wanted to be with me anymore.

When we landed, would he leave with them and go somewhere else?

"All right, all right. First thing is first—we need to hide. Any idea where a good place would be?"

I bit my lip. I knew it would be a stupid idea, but it would make it so they couldn't leave me behind. "What if we went to the Sirian Zone?"

They all stared at me as if I were crazy. Maybe they didn't want me to tag along. My fears were right.

Ellie let out a breath. "Well, I doubt Byron would be able to find us easily there, but Sirians... They don't like our kind. At all. I have been chased away from their zone many times."

"They will let you in, don't you worry," I said as I tapped my finger on the glass of my drink. "Because my mother is the leader of the Sirians."

***

Acknowledgements

I want to say thank you to everyone who made this possible. First off, my husband who "gets the pleasure" of reading all my stories multiple times and has always stayed by my side and pushed me forward.

Also, my parents and family who have supported me since the beginning. To all my friends who get to put up with me talking about my characters, the research I find, and just getting asked the most random questions. Special thank you to my writing group and writing instructors/mentors who have always supported me and believed in me.

A special thanks to my editors at Victory Editing, the artist for this cover WHO DID A FANTASTIC JOB, Mona Finden, and a thanks to Biserka Designs for formatting and adding the title.

Lastly, thank you to my readers for supporting me by buying my books. I wouldn't be here without you!

Dani Hoots is a young adult sci-fi and fantasy author that likes to be inspired by ancient tales. She has a background in anthropology, urban planning, herbal science, and sci-fi writing. She enjoys reading about history, astronomy and plants, and in her spare time she is either watching anime, reading manga and books, or drawing. Check out her website for a FREE *City of Kaus* novella!
www.DaniHoots.com
Feel free to email her with any questions you might have!
danihootsauthor@gmail.com